The Secret Admirer: A Deadly Obsession

Ny'Kole Cereza

Witches o Words

Contents

Prolonge

Aurora

Today was another horrible day. It was raining all day, and some streets were flooded. As I trudged through the rain- soaked streets, my mind kept going back to the case I was working on. The chilling details of the case haunted me, pushing me to dig deeper and uncover the dark secrets hidden within. I pushed the door open to the precinct. The moment I stepped inside, the familiar scent of coffee and paperwork enveloped me, grounding me in the reality of my job. As I made my way to my desk, I knew that today would be another long day.

I sigh, sit down, and stretch my legs, thinking about today's case again. Another violent crime. Domestic violence. senseless murder. The victim was a young mother, leaving behind two children. It breaks my heart to see the impact of these heinous acts on innocent lives.

Despite the darkness of the situation, we were able to catch the bad guy. He killed his wife because she wanted a divorce. She wanted her kids to be free from his violent ways. Justice was served, but it was bittersweet knowing that those children would grow up without their mother. The cycle of violence had been broken, but the scars left behind would last a lifetime.

Looking at my desk, I notice a vase with purple roses in it. The delicate petals of the rose are beginning to wilt, hinting at its age. The rich purple color stands out against the stark white walls of my office.

"When did this get here?" I thought. I must have received it as a gift recently, but I can't remember when I got it. When I searched the vase, there was a card attached. It read, "Roses are purple, violets are blue. Your beauty is fleeting, but my love will always pursue you. Anonymous." What the fuck? I racked my brain, trying to think of who could have sent me such a mysterious gift. The note only added to the intrigue, leaving me with more questions than answers.

"This is too fucked up." I whispered. I picked up the vase and was going to throw it in the trash next to my desk, but my witchy senses started tingling. Or, was it my detective senses? Either way, this just screams weird. I will take them down to the lab and see if they can get anything off the roses or note. Or, maybe there's some sort of clue hidden in the vase that could help me figure out what's going on. It's worth investigating further before just tossing it aside. Who would go through the trouble of sending me roses with such a cryptic message? There's definitely more to this than meets the eye. I need to dig deeper and unravel this mystery before making any hasty decisions. It's time to put my investigative skills to the test and see where this strange gift leads me.

"Aurora McCoy. Just the girl I was looking for." Director Javier Martinez says: or, as I call him, Uncle Javier. He is my mother's eldest brother. He almost got a punch in the face while dragging me out of my thoughts. He should know better than to startle me like that.

Where are my manners? I just remembered that I have not introduce myself. My name is Aurora McCoy. I am a curvaceous woman of mixed heritage; my features are a blend of African American, Spanish, and Irish. Standing tall at 5'10' with a confident stride, I carry myself with the grace of a dancer despite my size 24 frame. As a human and witch, there's a subtle power that surrounds me—a hint of something beyond the ordinary in my deep eyes.

My face is heart-shaped, a canvas of warmth and strength, with high cheekbones that speak to my Spanish roots. My nose is broad and slightly flared, a testament to my African ancestry, while my full lips, often adorned with a dark vampire shade, curve into a smile that can disarm even the most hardened criminal. My ears, pointed at the tips, are a subtle nod to my magical heritage, a whisper of the secrets they've heard on the wind.

One hazel. One green. My curly hair, a wild mane of crimson and copper hues, seems to have a life of its own, echoing the untamed magic that flows through my veins. Unfortunately, there are limitations to my abilities. My coven's elders have placed a limiter on my abilities because they worry that if I fully embrace all of my powers, chaos may result. Being a half witch, half human hybrid, my powers require a delicate balance of control. My mother was the most powerful type of witch—an elemental. She possessed an extraordinary level of power, which she graciously bestowed upon me.

I have spent years honing my skills and learning to control the unpredictable nature of my magic. While some of my powers are still accessible to me, I must tread carefully. The elders have warned me of the dangers of losing control, emphasizing the importance of restraint and responsibility in wielding my magic. Luckily, I still have access to what I call "everyday witch abilities," like minor spellcasting and energy manipulation. Let's not forget my witchy senses.

"No. Whatever it is, no." I replied. I just know he is going to try to give me another case. "By the way, Director, did you see anyone put purple roses on my desk?"

"No, I haven't seen anyone put purple roses on your desk," my uncle replied with a puzzled expression. I couldn't help but wonder who could have left such a mysterious gift for me. Could it be a secret admirer or perhaps a warning from an unknown source? The purple roses seemed to hold a message waiting to be unraveled. "Where are they?"

"They are behind me. I had a feeling I should take them down to the lab and see if they could pull anything from them. There was a cryptic ass message left with them too." I said with a pointed look. My uncle knew exactly what I meant by feeling. I quickly retrieved the roses from the desk behind me and showed them to my uncle. He read the message out loud: "Roses are purple, violets are blue. Your beauty is fleeting, but my love will always pursue you. Anonymous." My heart raced as I tried to decipher the meaning behind the ominous words.

"That is a bit creepy, Aurora. Do you want me to look into it?" He asked.

"If you have time, sure. I don't know who could have left this message, but it might be worth investigating." My uncle reassured me that he would investigate discreetly, and I couldn't help but feel grateful for his support in this unsettling situation.

"I will take it to the lab and have it analyzed. When I know something, you will." He says.

"Now that the distraction is gone, tell me what you want." I command.

"Relax, Aurora. I just wanted to commend you on your work with the recent case." Uncle Javier says it with a smile.

"Now, cut the BS, boss. What do you have for me?" I ask, crossing my arms in front of me. I know there's no way he's being nice for no reason.

"We have a case that I need you to look into. I know you just got done with a hard one, and I wouldn't be asking if I didn't need my best on this." Uncle Javier says, handing me a file with a knowing look. I take the file and begin to skim through it, already feeling the familiar rush of adrenaline that comes with a new investigation. As I read through the details, I felt disgusted. I have seen some horrible crime scenes, but this one takes the cake. The case involved a string of gruesome murders that seemed to be connected in some way. There are ten victims between the ages of eighteen and twenty-eight. The brutality of the crimes made my blood run cold. The killer left no evidence behind, making it a challenging case. I knew this would be a test of my skills like never before. Uncle Javier was right; this was definitely my kind of case.

"Do I have too?" I questioned.

Uncle Javier smiled and said, "You have a knack for solving the most complex cases and bringing justice to those who need it." I nodded, feeling determined to uncover the truth behind these heinous crimes.

"I will look into it. However, this is going to take up a lot of my time." I informed him.

Uncle Javier nodded understandingly. "I trust you will prioritize this case. We need your expertise on this."

"I don't like this," I tell him, shaking the case file. The file was light—too light.

Uncle Javier raised an eyebrow and asked, "What do you mean?"

I explained, "There's barely any evidence in here. It's almost as if someone wanted to make this case impossible to solve."

Uncle Javier's expression turned grave. "This just got a lot more complicated."

"Complicated doesn't even begin to explain this shit," I replied.

"We need to dig deeper and find out who's trying to sabotage this investigation," Uncle Javier said firmly. I nodded in agreement, knowing that this case was going to require all of my skills and determination.

"I don't like this," I repeat.

"I know. You are one of the best we have. I need you on this, Ro." He sighs. He was calling me by my nickname. He only does it when he is stressed out. "We can't let whoever is behind this get away with it," Uncle Javier added, his eyes narrowing in determination.

"I said I would do it," I told him. Uncle Javier nodded, his expression showing a mix of relief and confidence in my abilities.

"Good," he said. "Let's get to work and bring justice to those responsible for this mess." With a sense of purpose, I knew that this investigation was going to push me to my limits, but I was ready to take on the challenge. "Oh, this will be a joint investigation with the FBI."

I suddenly snapped my head up, shooting him a fierce glare as I firmly declared, "No way. I prefer to work alone. Reluctantly, I join the team, but I do not do partners. You know that."

Uncle Javier chuckled, seemingly unfazed by my outburst. "Yes, they'll be assisting us on this case. It's a big one."

"Assisting? More like meddling and trying to take all the credit," I muttered under my breath. My heart raced at the thought of collaborating with those egotistical, by-the-book agents who always seemed to think they knew better than local law enforcement.

"Aurora," Uncle Javier said, his tone firm but understanding. "I know you prefer working solo, but this case requires a partner. A team effort. Trust me, we need all the help we can get."

I crossed my arms defiantly and said, "Uncle Javier, I've handled plenty of big cases on my own. I don't need the FBI breathing down my neck and questioning my every move." He raised an eyebrow at me, a hint of amusement in his eyes.

"You're calling me 'Uncle Javier' now? Are you trying to guilt-trip me?" I scoffed, "Hardly. Just stating facts." I took a deep breath, trying to reign in my frustration. I knew Uncle Javier had a point, but the idea of working with the FBI still rankled me. I knew I had to swallow my pride and accept the help, even if it meant sacrificing some independence.

Deep down, I understood that collaboration with the FBI could be crucial in solving this case.

"Fine," I said through gritted teeth, "but if those agents get in my way, they'll answer to me."

Uncle Javier smiled, knowing he had won this battle. "You'll meet them tomorrow. Try to play nice, Aurora."

"Never." I grumbled a half-hearted agreement and waved him off, already dreading the inevitable clash of personalities that awaited me. "Fine. Let me be."

With a sense of responsibility weighing on my shoulders and a growing resentment towards the impending collaboration, I began diving into the case file, ready to face the challenges ahead, both in the investigation and with the FBI. I turned on the police radio, the familiar chatter a small comfort in the face of the daunting task ahead. With each new piece of information I uncovered from the file, I knew this was going to be one of my most complex cases to date. As I sifted through the evidence, I realized that everything was a mess.

The suspects' alibis didn't add up, and the timeline was all over the place. It was clear that untangling this web of deceit was going to require all of my skills and determination. The more I delved into the case, the more complexities and twists I uncovered, making me see the gravity of the situation at hand. It was clear that untangling this web of deceit would require all of my skills and determination. I was so focused on the case file that the crackle of the radio jolted me back to reality.

Dispatch crackled over the radio, "All units, we have a 10-54 at the old mill. Please respond."

A voice cut through the static. It sounded like Officer Davis. "10-4, Dispatch. Unit 23 en route, ETA five minutes."

A second later, a different voice chimed in, "Dispatch, this is Unit 7. We're closer; we're already passing Main Street. Be there in two."

Dispatch acknowledged: "10-4, Units 7 and 23. Be advised, potential 10-57 on scene. The victim is a young female, a possible connection to the ongoing investigation."

The first officer responded grimly, "Copy that, dispatch. We'll proceed with caution."

"Dispatch, this is Detective McCoy. I will join. Request permission to assist."

There was a pause, and then Dispatch responded, "10-4, Detective McCoy. Permission granted. Proceed with caution and keep us updated."

My heart raced as I grabbed my keys and rushed out the door, knowing that this new development could be the key to unraveling the mystery. As I sped towards the old mill, my mind raced with the possibilities of what awaited me there. The adrenaline was already pumping through my veins, a familiar feeling I both dreaded and craved. The thought of another victim, potentially linked to the ongoing case, sent a chill down my spine.

As I neared the scene, I could see flashing lights cutting through the twilight. The old mill, a relic of the town's past, loomed ominously in the distance. I took a deep breath, bracing myself for whatever I might find inside.

Chapter 1

Aurora

The old mill. I remember this place. It was the desinated necking spot. Teens and young couples would come up here to steal a moment alone, away from prying eyes. The sound of the water rushing by always added to the romantic atmosphere of the old mill. Dragging me to a memory of a younger me spinning around in a yellow dress, he was sitting on the old stump with laughter in his eyes. The old mill held the secrets of my young love and innocence, forever preserved in its weathered walls. I think the last time I was here was when I just turned twenty-three. He thought it would be funny to come up here again, like when we were younger.

Dragging myself out of memory lane, I couldn't have prepared myself more for what I discovered within. The scene was a bloody mess. The walls were splattered with crimson streaks, and the floor was slick with blood. It was a gruesome sight that made my stomach churn.

I pulled up at the same time as Detective Mike Ashley and his current trainee, Officer Jenny Jones. Detective Ashley is a long time vet, and I trust his experience and instincts in situations like this. However, when it comes to Officer Jones, I cannot trust Detective Ashley's judgment. She was new to homicide and still had a lot to learn. But there was something about her that I just didn't trust. My senses were tingling. Maybe it was her nervous demeanor or the way she avoided eye contact with me. She bore a striking resemblance to me. Similar but different. We could be sisters if it weren't for our different hair and eye colors. She always covers half her face with her hair. Either way, I couldn't shake the feeling that she was hiding something.

As we continued to investigate the crime scene, I made a mental note to keep a close eye on Officer Jones. Walking further into the room, I could see Officer Jones Davis and his partner, Officer John Lawson, were already inside. I could hear them discussing the details of the crime scene; their expressions were grim.

As I approached, Officer Davis turned to me and said, "You're going to want to brace yourself for this one."

"That bad?" I asked.

Officer Lawson nodded solemnly, his eyes fixed on the gruesome scene in front of us. "The worst one we've seen in a while," he added quietly. I took a deep breath and mentally prepared myself for what lay ahead.

"Detective McCoy. Detective Ashley. Its good to see you, despite the circumstances," Officer Davis said, his voice heavy with concern. "Which one of you will be leading the case."

"Detective McCoy got here first. Just think of us as backup." Detective Ashley says. "If you don't mind us staying and observing, we might be able to offer some insight or assistance. Plus, Officer Jones needs the experience."

I nodded in agreement, appreciating the extra support. "We can use all the help we can get on this one," I replied, gesturing for them to follow as they began to investigate the crime scene together.

"We'll fill you both in on the details as we go through the evidence," Officer Lawson added, gesturing for me to follow them further into the crime scene.

"Let's take a look at the scene first. From what I have seen, there is a lot to take in." I replied.

"How about Officer Jones takes a look around the perimeter while Detective McCoy and I start examining the evidence?" Detective Ashley suggested, looking at me, wanting to divide and conquer the investigation efficiently.

I nodded my head in agreement. "Good suggestion."

As we began to piece together the clues, I couldn't help but feel grateful for the extra hands on deck. The more eyes we had on the evidence, the better chance we had of solving this case quickly. I knew that with everyone's expertise combined, we would be able to bring justice to the victim and their family. Together, we meticulously combed through the crime scene, analyzing every detail for potential leads. Each piece of evidence brought could bring us closer to uncovering the truth behind this heinous crime.

I closed my eyes, took a deep breath, and opened my energy field. Nothing changed in my outward appearance, but I was now able to see beyond the physical realm. The subtle energies surrounding the crime scene began to reveal themselves to me, providing a new perspective that could be crucial in solving the case.

There was one problem. There was no evidence. Not even my energy field could pick up something. Despite how bloody the scene was, there was nothing there. The lack of evidence was puzzling, leading me to consider the possibility of a staged crime scene. It became clear that I needed to think outside the box and explore alternative avenues to crack this case.

Walking around the crime scene, I finally stopped at the victim. A young woman, barely out of her teens, lies lifeless on the ground. Naked. I could tell her innocence was lost. Her body was bloody yet clean. My eyes, picking up the energy around her body, sensed a strange aura, as if there was some sort of presence lingering. It was then that I realized this case may involve more than just physical evidence, prompting me to delve deeper into the supernatural aspects surrounding the crime.

As I looked closer, I noticed a faint glimmer of something shiny near her hand. It was a small, delicate necklace that seemed out of place in the chaos surrounding her. Could this be the key to unlocking the mystery behind her tragic death?

"Shit. She looks young." I muttered to myself, feeling a surge of anger towards whoever could have done this to her.

"She is according to her driver's license. Her name is Ashley Arms. Twenty-three years old as of yesterday." Officer Davis comments.

"She was almost a kid," I say, my heart sinking at the thought of such a young life being taken so brutally.

"She is just a few years younger than you. Stop acting like you are fifty. But we do need to find whoever did this and make sure they pay for what they've done." Officer Davis said with determination in his voice.

"She might not have been here alone given what this place represents." I comment.

"Your right. I once caught my son up here." Detective Ashley replies.

"Detective McCoy. Come look at this." Officer Lawson called out to me, breaking me out of my thoughts. I turned to see him pointing at a piece of evidence that could crack the case wide open. My heart raced with a mix of anticipation and dread as I stepped closer to take a look. A fucking paw print. This case wasn't going to be hard enough.

"Wild animal?" I asked, hopefully. Knowing damn well that it wasn't. It was too big to be a regular animal. This is terrible news.

"I am not sure. We would need an expert to tell the difference." Officer Lawson replied. I felt a sinking feeling in my stomach as I realized the implications of finding a paw print at the crime scene. This just added another layer of complexity to an already challenging investigation.

"Call it in, Officer Lawson. We have to know." I ordered. Officer Lawson nodded and pulled out his phone to make the call. The re-alization that we were dealing with something much more dangerous than initially thought settled in, making me even more determined to solve this case.

"We need to be prepared for anything," I thought to myself as I watched Officer Lawson make the call. The urgency of the situation was now crystal clear, and we needed to act fast to ensure the safety of everyone involved.

It took less than 30 minutes for the expert to come. As we briefed the expert on the situation, I couldn't shake the feeling of unease that lingered in the air. The gravity of the situation weighed heavily on my mind as we awaited their assessment. If this was what I thought it was, this case just got worse.

The expert's expression grew serious as they listened to our account, almost confirming my worst fears. I knew we had to trust the expert's judgment and follow their recommendations closely. Time was of the essence, and any misstep could have serious consequences. As we waited for their assessment, I braced myself for whatever news they had to deliver.

"You were right to call us." Zane Carter comments. He part of the local wolf pack and a forensic expert. "Judging by the size of the paw and the depth of the claw marks, I'd say we're dealing with a large predator here." My heart sank at the confirmation, knowing that we were facing a dangerous threat. A threat so destructive that it required immediate action to ensure everyone's safety.

"Shit, it is what I expected. We have a killer werewolf on our hands." I said, trying to keep my voice steady despite the fear creeping in. Zane nodded grimly, signaling that we needed to act fast before more lives were put at risk.

"You're going to have to get the local Alpha involved." Zane gives me a pointed look. I knew he was right. Involving the Alpha was the only way to handle a threat of this magnitude and ensure the safety of our town.

"The pack needs to be warned," Zane added, his expression grave. I nodded in agreement, knowing that involving the Alpha of the local pack was crucial to handling the situation effectively. There is only one problem: I fucking hate his guts.

Caleb Nichols. Caleb was an imposing figure, a towering 6'9" of pure muscle and raw power. As the local Alpha of the Wolf Pack, his presence exuded an air of dominance that few dared to challenge. His chiseled features, sharp jawline, and piercing blue eyes hinted at the feral nature that lay beneath his human facade. Thick, dark hair, often worn long and loose, framed his face, while a dusting of stubble accentuated his rugged masculinity. He is the bane of my existence. And the once love of my life. Despite my personal feelings towards Caleb, I knew that the safety of the people was the top priority. Swallowing my pride, I agreed to involve him.

"Who wants to do the honors?" I asked sarcastically, knowing full well that I would be making that call. As expected, no one volunteered, so I took a deep breath and dialed Caleb's number. It was easy to find his number. It was still saved in my phone under "Asshole Ex." The sooner we solve this case, the better chance we have of preventing any potential danger. And the less likely it is for me to go to jail for manslaughter.

After a few rings, he picked up, his voice still as annoyingly deep as ever. "What do you want?" he asked, his tone dripping with sleep.

"Alpha Caleb Nichols, this is Detective Aurora McCoy." I began to say but was cut off.

"I know who this is, or did my question not give it away?" He replied. I take it he is still mad at me for what happen. For what I done. But who cares that doesn't give him the right to speak to me like that.

"And what makes you think I care?" I snapped.

"Detective McCoy, we need his help, remember." Officer Lawson said. I took a deep breath and tried to calm myself before continuing.

"Alpha Nichols, we need your Expertise on this case. It's urgent." I manage to say nicely.

Caleb sighed heavily on the other end of the line before finally responding, "Expertise, huh? Fine, I'll hear you out. Just remember, I'm not in the business of doing favors for cops, so this better be good."

"We appreciate your willingness to help, Alpha Nichols. We believe your unique skills can make a difference in solving this case." I said, hoping to appeal to his sense of pride and Expertise.

Caleb chuckled before replying, "Alright, I'll bite. Tell me what you've got, Aurora."

"A dead body and a werewolf footprint," I informed him.

Caleb's laughter abruptly stopped, replaced by a tense silence. After a moment, he muttered, "Lucky for you, I will be there in an hour."

"What do you mean?" I questioned.

"Your director called in for our help on a case." He responds. The only people the director called in were the FBI. I felt a chill run down my spine at the realization.

"You work for the FBI?" I asked, feeling a mix of pain and anger.

"Yes." He replied. I couldn't believe that Caleb, my ex-boyfriend, was now working for the FBI. The thought of having to work with him again made my stomach churn. The revelation sent a jolt through me, a cold dread seeping into my bones. Caleb Nichols, my former flame and the source of countless sleepless nights, wasn't just the enigmatic leader of the local werewolf pack; he was also a Special Agent with the FBI. The news was both a shock and a gut punch, a stark reminder of the man's complex nature and the secrets he held close to his chest. Secrets he kept from me.

Flashbacks flooded my mind, vivid fragments of our shared past. I remembered the stolen glances, the whispered promises, and the stolen kisses beneath the full moon. Our love had been a whirlwind, a passionate dance of desire and danger. But it had also been fraught with conflict and misunderstandings, our differing worlds colliding with explosive force.

I had always been drawn to Caleb's demanding presence, his tamed energy that didn't mirror the untamed magic flowing through my veins. But our relationship had been doomed from the start, a star-crossed love affair that was never meant to be. Caleb's loyalty to his pack and his duty as the heir often put him at odds with my pursuit of freedom, creating a rift that ultimately tore us apart.

Yet, despite the pain and heartache, I couldn't deny the lingering connection I felt towards Caleb. He was a man of contradictions, a wolf in sheep's clothing, a protector, and a predator all rolled into one. And now, as I stood on the precipice of a new investigation, one that delved into the murky depths of the supernatural world, I found myself paired with him once again.

Breaking out of thought, I replied, "I see."

Caleb's presence brought a mix of emotions: familiarity, distrust, and a hint of unresolved feelings. As we embarked on this new case together, I couldn't help but wonder if our past would hinder or help our investigation.

"I suppose we'll have to put our differences aside for the sake of this case," I said, trying to ignore the memories of our past conflicts resurfacing.

"We will." He said.

"I will see you then," I replied, disregarding the pain I felt.

Chapter 2

Caleb

Today, I started off as a typical day. However, I felt like something needed to be fixed. As I went about my usual routine, a sense of unease lingered in the back of my mind. Little did I know, a series of unexpected events would soon unfold, turning my day upside down.

I was working on an investigation into a missing person case. A child. He was just 5 years old. He went missing in front of his home. He was playing with a friend when he disappeared. The parents were distraught, and the community was in a state of panic. The police had been searching for him for days with no luck. So, they called us in. The FBI. My partner and I arrived at the scene and immediately began combing through the area for any clues. The pressure was on us to find the child and bring him home safely.

As I delved deeper into the case, I uncovered some unsettling clues that pointed towards a possible abduction. Blood. We quickly secured the area and collected the evidence for analysis, hoping it would lead us to the missing child. Time was of the essence as we worked tirelessly to piece together what had happened to him.

I was going through the case file when I received a tip that led me to a surprising breakthrough. As I followed up on the lead, I uncovered new evidence that could potentially solve the case and bring closure to the victim's family. The information I gathered pointed towards a possible suspect, and I immediately contacted the authorities to share my findings. One man was in every picture taken near the scene of the crime. This new development gave us a strong lead to pursue in our investigation. As we delved deeper into the suspect's background, we discovered a pattern of behavior that aligned with the details of the case. The pieces were finally starting to fall into place, and it seemed like we were getting closer to solving the mystery.

We had him brought in for questioning, and he folded. He told us he took the boy because he looked like his dead son. He wasn't going to hurt him. The man's confession provided us with a clear motive for the crime, shedding light on his actions. Despite the unusual circumstances, we were able to bring the missing boy back to safety and close the case.

I began to make my way back to the office. As I drove, I couldn't help but feel a sense of relief, knowing that we had successfully resolved the case and brought the boy home unharmed. But I still had that sense of dread. Like something was left unfinished or something terrible was about to happen.

As I parked my car and entered the office, I couldn't shake this feeling of unease. I continued on with my routine. I locked up my gun and debriefed with my team, but the sense of unease lingered.

"Caleb, are you good?" Jason Giles asked. Jason is my partner. My right hand, man. I smiled and nodded, not wanting to burden him with my worries. But deep down, I knew that something was still off, and I couldn't shake the feeling of impending doom. It was going to be a long night.

"Naw, man, something is wrong." He persisted.

"You ever have a gut feeling that won't go away?" I hesitated before finally admitting it. "Like, something just doesn't feel right."

"I might have had it once or twice." Jason admitted. "Normally goes away for me."

"I cannot shake it." I replied shaking my head.

"Caleb, Jason, to my office." FBI Director Barnes called out. My heart sank as I followed Jason to the director's office, wondering what new trouble awaited us. As we entered the office, Director Barnes fixed us with a serious gaze and said, "We have a situation that requires your immediate attention." My stomach churned with unease as I braced myself for whatever was coming our way. "You are to pack up immediately; you are going home, boys."

I exchanged a confused glance with Jason before turning back to Director Barnes, who continued, "We have a possible serial killer in Ohio. Your Expertise is needed to assist with the investigation. You will be working with the detective in charge. Get ready; your flight leaves in two hours."

My mind raced with thoughts of the dangerous task ahead as we quickly gathered our belongings and prepared for the journey to Ohio.

"I will meet you there." I tell Jason.

"Luke giving you a ride." He asks.

"No. Luke is on vacation. Haven't heard from him lately." I commented walking away.

"Wait. Do you think this is what you were feeling?" Jason asks.

I nod and walk away, a sense of foreboding settling in the pit of my stomach. Director Barnes's urgency only confirmed my suspicions—this would be a challenging and potentially life-threatening case. I haven't been to Ohio in years, not since Aurora. Aurora McCoy. My ex-girlfriend and the one who got away. Memories of her came flooding back, reminding me of the long hours and sleepless nights spent with her.

I drove home to pack and get ready. As I packed my bags, I couldn't shake the feeling that this case would bring back memories I had long buried. Memories of Aurora and the pain of losing her. Despite the uncertainty, I knew I had to face this challenge head-on.

Leaving to board the plane, I made a silent promise to stay focused on the task and not let personal emotions cloud my judgment. I must keep a clear mind to solve this case and rely on my training and experience. The past was catching up to me, and I had a sinking feeling that it wouldn't be long before everything unraveled. I shake my head, pushing away the memories as I focus on the task.

The plane ride was long and uncomfortable, but I used the time to review the case details and mentally prepare for what lay ahead. There are ten victims between the ages of 18 and 25. The killer left no evidence behind. As I landed in the city where the murders took place, I knew that time was of the essence in solving this case before another life was taken. With a deep breath, I stepped off the plane and headed back to Ohio.

As I arrived home dead tired, I went straight to the shower. The warm water helped to wash away the stress of the day, allowing my mind to relax and unwind. Afterward, I settled into bed, hoping that a good night's sleep would clarify the case.

I woke up with a start. The sound of my phone ringing next to me indicated that someone was calling me. As I reached for it, I couldn't shake the feeling that something important was about to happen.

"It was the middle of the night. Who could be calling?" I thought. Reluctantly, I looked at my caller ID and froze. The name on the screen was that of my ex-girlfriend. My heart raced as I answered the call, unsure of what she could want after all this time. I picked up the phone, my voice deep with sleep. The conversation begins with a tense exchange between Aurora and me.

Just listening to her talk makes my anger resurface. I couldn't help but respond sarcastically when she identified herself. It seems she needs help on a case, and she tries to appeal to my sense of duty and expertise. What the fuck does that even mean? Although I want to resist, I eventually agree to hear her out when she emphasizes the urgency of the situation.

What she says stops me in my tracks. Aurora reveals that the case involves a dead body and a werewolf footprint, implying that a werewolf might be responsible. One of my werewolves might be involved. She ends the conversation by saying we need to put our differences aside for the sake of this case. She was the one who broke up with me. She walked away from our relationship without a second thought. Despite my anger, I know that solving this case is more important than our past issues. .

I quickly hung up the phone, my mind racing with thoughts. A dead body, wolf footprints, and Aurora McCoy. A deadly combination. I don't know what is worse, but one thing is sure. Anything having to do with Aurora McCoy is trouble. She always seems to be involved in some dangerous investigation.

I grabbed my phone and called Jason. Jason is my beta in the pack. He answered on the first ring, his voice filled with concern.

"Aurora called." I said urgently.

"What? Wait, let me get up." He comments. "Are we talking about your Aurora?"

"She is not my anything, Jason." I snapped, frustration creeping into my voice. "But yes, that Aurora. She called, informing me that a body was found next to a set of wolf prints."

Jason's concern turned to alarm. "Wolf prints? That can't be good," he replied. "I'll meet you there." I hung up and headed out the door, knowing that trouble always seemed to find its way to Aurora McCoy. I knew I had to act fast before the situation escalated. With a deep breath, I gathered my things and headed out the door. I couldn't shake the feeling of unease that had settled in the pit of my stomach.

Chapter 3

Aurora

As I made my way back to the precinct, my thoughts kept drifting back to Caleb. I knew I wasn't going to get any sleep tonight. I'll be lucky to get another cup of coffee. Making the call to Caleb took more out of me than I would like to admit. We didn't end our relationship on good terms. It was explosive. I will admit, it was my fault. I broke up with him. I hurt him, but that doesn't give him the right to treat me like shit. I won't allow it.

Just the thought of him pisses me off. Almost as much as I hate criminals. I could feel my blood boiling just thinking about how things ended between us. I might have broken up with him, but it was still his fault. He was always putting his pack first. Long before he ascended to the position of Alpha. I stood by him when his father shattered his dreams. When no one believed in him, I was right there. When some of his pack would tease me and speak in wolf language behind my back, he did nothing to defend me.

Despite all my support and loyalty, he still chose to prioritize his pack over me. It was a painful realization that ultimately led to our breakup. His inability to fully commit to our relationship because of his loyalty to his pack was something I couldn't overlook. I was never mad at his commitment to his pack, I just wished he felt that our relationship was worth fighting for as well.

My anger was coming back, and so was the pain he left behind. But I knew I had to push those feelings aside and focus on the task at hand—catching the criminal who had been terrorizing our city.

Think Aurora. A werewolf. Judging by the footprints I saw, they had to be a Psi or an Omega, if i remember correctly. A Psi is usually a new or yearling wolf. An Omega is the lowest- ranking wolf. Their behavior is often erratic and unpredictable, making them a dangerous threat to society. Could any other rank be responsible? The scene was too bloody for a gamma or beta. What about an epsilon? No, they are best at fighting and subduing people.

Shaking my head. I arrived at the precinct and set my stuff down, I noticed more purple roses with the same note. I don't have time for this nonsense. I quickly scanned the room for any signs of who could be leaving them, but found nothing. This mysterious gesture was starting to feel like a distraction from my real work.

I picked the roses up and walked to the lab. I needed to focus on the case at hand, not some mysterious admirer. As I entered the lab, I hoped that analyzing the roses would provide some clue as to who was behind this strange gesture.

"Sam, just the woman I was looking for." I said this as I was opening the door to the lab. Samantha Grey. Our resident forensic genius. We went to high school together. She is one of the few people I trust and call a friend who works here. Sam looked up from her microscope with a curious expression on her face.

"What's going on?" she asked, clearly intrigued by my urgency.

I handed her the roses and said, "We have a mystery to solve."

"Wow. Purple roses. You don't see that every day." Sam replies. "A present for me?"

"You may dissect them to your heart's content, but I need you to see what you can pull for them." I informed her. "Someone is leaving them on my desk. They come with a creepy note."

"Roses are purple. Violets are blue. Your time is up. I'm coming for you." Sam's voice trailed off, a chill creeping into the air. "That's... disturbing," she finally said, her voice hushed. "And they're just leaving these on your desk?"

"This is the second time. Director is looking into it from his end, but his is swamped," I confirmed, my jaw clenching. "And it' has been a note attached to the same type of flower. It's starting to feel personal."

"We'll get to the bottom of this, Aurora," Sam assured me, her voice firm. "I'll have the flowers analyzed for any DNA or fingerprints."

I nodded, a grim determination settling over me. "Hopefully it is just someone playing a game. Thanks, Sam. I have to get back to my case."

"No problem. I got you." Sam patted my shoulder before I turned to leave her lab, my mind already racing with possible suspects.

As I walked back to my desk, I couldn't shake the feeling that this was just the beginning of something much bigger. I proceed to gather the team, and we try to come up with a plan to track down this werewolf before they strike again.

"Detective McCoy." Officer Lawson called. I turned to face him, ready to discuss our next move in tracking down the werewolf. When I realized why he called me, a familiar face walked into the conference room—the city's mayor. My heart sank as I realized this case was about to become even more complicated with political interference.

"Mayor Greg Daniels, as I live and breathe," I say this as he approaches me. Mayor Daniels is an old gamma. Gamma possesses a wealth of knowledge and experience, making them the pack's most seasoned and knowledgeable member. They share their Expertise by recounting tales for the next generation. Gammas (sometimes referred to as Elders) are highly respected individuals, mainly because many of them have held the position of alphas at some point in their lives. He was, unfortunately, living in a society where power dynamics are constantly shifting between humans and the supernatural; having a werewolf as the mayor wasn't difficult to understand, but overall, it was terrible for this case. Mayor Daniels was known for his ability to navigate the political landscape with finesse, but his presence at the crime scene raised suspicions about his motives.

As he greeted me with a knowing smile, I couldn't help but wonder what role he would play in this investigation. "Detective McCoy, I trust you are handling this investigation with the utmost discretion." He said smoothly. I knew then that this case would be a delicate dance between law enforcement and politics. "I hope you called this in." He adds with a particular look on his face.

"I assure you we were following protocol," I informed him. Mayor Daniels nodded, his expression unreadable, before excusing himself to speak with the director. His involvement in the investigation only added another layer of complexity to an already intricate case.

"This is bad, Detective McCoy." Officer Davis says.

"We need to tread carefully with the mayor involved." I replied, knowing that every move we made would be scrutinized. The pressure was on to solve this case smoothly.

"Now, who's coming in?" Officer Davis questions. I looked up just as he was getting out of the elevator. Caleb was here, and he brought Jason along. Just great. The mayor and Caleb are in the same room. Why me?

"Aurora," Caleb says.

"It's Detective McCoy." I replied. He doesn't get to call me by my name. Fucker.

"Right. How can I forget?" He says it nonchalantly. "Show me the body."

"You know that is not going to happen." I retorted. "I do, however, have permission to show you pictures."

I handed him the folder containing the crime scene photos, watching his expression closely as he flipped through them. Caleb's face remained impassive, but I could see a flicker of something in his eyes. "Interesting." He finally said, handing the folder back to me. "Let's discuss."

"What is there to discuss? One of your own may be involved with the murder of this woman. We must figure out who it is and bring them to justice." Caleb's expression darkened at my words; a sense of betrayal was evident in his eyes.

"I'll handle this internally." He said firmly. "You stay out of it."

"Like hell, I will. You don't get to decide how I handle my murder investigation, especially since it may involve one of your own. I, unfortunately, was told we need to work together to solve this before it's too late." Caleb's jaw was clenched, not liking the idea of us working together. "Not to mention, this case may be linked to ten other victims. We must put our differences aside and focus on finding the killer before they strike again." I continued, trying to appeal to Caleb's sense of duty. Caleb reluctantly nodded, realizing the gravity of the situation and the importance of cooperation in solving the case.

"Fine." He finally relented; his tone clipped. "But I call the shots."

I was about to lay it on him. He doesn't get to tell me what to do. I held my ground, knowing we needed to work together as equals to catch the killer. Caleb may have reservations, but I was determined to prove myself and solve the case alongside him.

"Great, you two met already." Uncle Javier says. "Let's get started on this case right away." Caleb and I exchanged a wary glance, knowing that our partnership would be challenging.

"What do you mean, unc, Director," I questioned. Almost calling him uncle.

"Sir?" Caleb interjected, his tone already bristling with impatience.

"She still has trouble calling me director instead of uncle. You two will be working closely with me on this case." Uncle Javier says. "Now, now. Detective McCoy. This is the special agent I told you would be working with on the potential serial killer case. I mean, you two will make a great team. Caleb's experience and your intuition will complement each other perfectly."

"This is not going to work. I work alone." I comment.

"Detective McCoy, this is a high-profile case that requires a collaborative effort," Uncle Javier explains again. "And I don't want you working this case alone. Trust me, Aurora, Special Agent Caleb is one of the best in the field. You said you would handle it."

"Great! Throw my words back at me. Don't expect me to play nice." I said, shaking my head. Uncle Javier nods in approval, knowing that, despite my initial resistance, I will do whatever it takes to catch the killer.

"Perfect!" He says. "Special Agent Caleb, I hope you two can put your differences aside and work together to solve this case efficiently."

"I'll do my best," He raised an eyebrow, clearly challenging me to say otherwise.

"Fine, but I'll be keeping a close eye on things," I replied, knowing our partnership would be a delicate balance of trust and suspicion. As we began strategizing our next steps, it was clear that our shared goal of justice would ultimately guide us through the investigation.

As we sat down to review the evidence, I couldn't shake the feeling that Caleb knew more than he was letting on. His calm demeanor only added to my suspicions. I needed to tread carefully to get to the bottom of this case. Even after everything we've been through, could I trust him? I closely watched Caleb's every move during our discussion, looking for any subtle signs of deception. It was clear that unraveling this mystery would require more than just the evidence in front of us. I needed to rely on my instincts and intuition to navigate this complex situation with Caleb.

Chapter 4

Caleb

Just seeing Aurora again made my blood boil. Her familiar scent of cinnamon, vanilla, and moonlight, which had haunted my dreams for years, wafted through the air, pulling me back to a time of youthful passion and raw vulnerability. My wolf stirred within me, a low growl rumbling in my chest as my eyes locked on her the other day. Aurora McCoy.

She was even more breathtaking than I remembered. Her curves, once a source of insecurity for her, are now a testament to her strength and resilience. Her honey-colored skin glowed under the dim office lights, and her eyes, filled with fiery intelligence, hinted at the pain we had both endured.

I had tried to forget her, burying myself in work, the responsibilities of leading the pack, and my work in the FBI. I drowned myself in whiskey on many nights, longing for her and hating her. But seeing her again, the memories flooded back— the laughter, the stolen kisses, the whispered promises of forever. My wolf whimpered, a longing echo of my own unspoken desires.

Aurora was a force of nature, a whirlwind of passion and determination. She had constantly challenged me and pushed me to be a better man, a better Alpha. Even when my family didn't approve of her, Aurora is not a wolf, and my parents, no, my father, disapproved. She comes from magic instead. And even now, as she stood before me, her chin held high, and her eyes narrowed in suspicion, I felt a thrill of excitement, a spark of the old flame that had never indeed died.

I knew this case would be complicated, both professionally and personally. The tension between us was palpable, a mix of unresolved feelings and the weight of our shared past. But I also knew that I couldn't stay away. Aurora was my mate, my other half, and the pull towards her was more potent than any sense of duty or self-preservation.

As I approached her, my every step radiating confidence and a hint of vulnerability, I couldn't help but smile. This was Aurora, my Aurora, the woman who had stolen my heart and left an emptiness in her wake. As our eyes met and a silent conversation passed between us, I knew that this was just the beginning of a new chapter filled with danger, passion, and the possibility of a love that could transcend the boundaries of time and circumstance.

But am I ready for it?

"Caleb, are we seriously going in?" Jason asked. Jarring me out of my thoughts. I looked up at him and nodded, determination shining in my eyes.

"We have too," I replied. "We must find out what is going on, and he may have answers."

"Do you think he will tell you?" Jason questioned. "Can we trust him not to say anything?"

"One thing my father will do is protect the pack." I say it grimly. "We have to take the risk. Let's go."

Even though I said those words, I am not sure. But I know that the only way to find out the truth is to confront my father, no matter how difficult it may be. The weight of the unknown hangs heavy on my shoulders as we make our way towards the pack territory. As we approach, I can feel the tension building in the air. I spotted my father sipping tea next to the fire, his gaze cold and calculating.

My father was the alpha before me. Though a century had passed since his birth, he bore the marks of time with surprising grace. His fur, more salt than pepper now, still held a healthy sheen, and his eyes, though lined with the wisdom of countless seasons, sparkled with a vitality that belied his years. He moved with a deliberate purpose, a hint of the powerful stride he once commanded still evident in his step. His posture remained ramrod straight, a testament to his enduring strength and the respect he commanded. While the pack recognized his age, they also saw the fire that still burned within him, a fire that fueled his passion for his people and his unwavering dedication to their well-being. His spirit remained as youthful and vibrant as ever, a beacon of hope and resilience for the pack.

He was by himself, which was good. Nobody will know I came in today. I took a deep breath, steeling myself for what was to come. It was time to finally confront him and uncover the secrets that had been hidden for so long.

"Father, I need to speak with you." I tell him. His eyes narrow as he looks at me, a flicker of surprise crossing his face before he schools his expression into one of indifference.

"What is it, son?" he replies, his voice low and controlled. I knew this conversation would not be easy, but I was determined to get the answers I had been seeking for so long.

"Not here," I manage to say. Even if he was no longer my Alpha, his energy still commanded respect and authority. He lost all althority over me when I became the Alpha of the pack. But the bond between us was still strong.

"Fine," he concedes, leading me to a secluded spot where we could speak privately. As we sat facing each other, the tension between us was palpable, a silent battle of wills waiting to unfold. I took out a magic stone. The stone will ensure that no one hears our conversation. I placed it between us, activating its power with a whisper of my energy. Now we could speak freely without fear of being overheard.

"What I say here doesn't leave this room." I finally tell him.

"It must be important if you need a secret stone." He says.

"It is important enough that I need you to swear on you, Alpha." I replied. The tension in the room thickened as he considered my request, his expression unreadable. Finally, he nodded solemnly.

"Consider it done," he said, placing his hand over his heart. "I swear as an Alpha that your words are safe with me." With that oath, I knew our conversation would remain confidential.

"Thank you. Father, I am here not just as the Alpha but as an agent." I began to reveal the true reason for my visit, knowing that I could trust him with this sensitive information. His eyes widened in surprise.

"Now, look here, Calab. I will not speak to any FBI agent even if he is my son." My father was visibly upset, but I knew I had to convince him that my intentions were pure.

"I promise you, Father, this is a matter of utmost importance to our pack. I need your help. I would never jeopardize our pack, you know that," I pleaded, hoping to appeal to his sense of duty and loyalty.

"I am listening," he said. I realized that was exactly how I treated Aurora when she called me. I took a deep breath, trying to gather my thoughts before continuing.

"I received a call from Detective Aurora McCoy. There was a murder of a young girl. Next to her body were wolf prints." I informed him. His eyes narrowed when I said Aurora's name but shifted when he realized the importance behind her call.

"You still talk to that girl?" He questioned.

"That is not important. But, no. This is the first time I have heard from her since we broke up." I answered truthfully. "She called me the Alpha. Not for any other reason."

"Humph. I don't like her, but we need to investigate this murder. We can't allow any human to look into our pack business." I could see the conflict in his eyes, torn between his dislike of Aurora and his duty to the pack. "What do you need?

"If I get you dates, can you secretively find out who wasn't with the pack on those dates? I asked, trying to find a compromise that would satisfy both his personal feelings and his responsibility to the pack.

"I'll do it," he finally agreed, with a reluctant nod. "Now leave. I need to focus and come up with a plan." With that, I left him to his thoughts, knowing that he would do what needed to be done for the good of the pack. As I walked away, I couldn't help but feel a sense of relief that he had agreed to help. Despite his reservations, I knew he would do whatever it took to protect the pack. I grabbed Jason on the way.

"Let's go." I said, leading him towards the exit. Jason nodded in understanding.

"He agreed?" Jason asked.

"He will help. I don't know how much." I replied. "We will find out."

As we made our way out of the den, I couldn't shake the feeling of uncertainty that lingered in the air. I knew that our next steps would be crucial in ensuring the safety of our pack, and I could only hope that our efforts would be enough to overcome the challenges ahead. The weight of responsibility settled on my shoulders as we ventured into the unknown, ready to face whatever obstacles came our way.

One thing is for sure: I will protect Aurora as well.

Chapter 5

- -

Aurora

Today was going to be a long day. I need to sit down and create a profile of the serial killer. This task will require all of my focus and attention to detail. Hopefully, by the end of the day, I'll better understand who we're dealing with. I'll start by compiling all our evidence and information so far. Then, I'll analyze his patterns and behaviors to predict his next move. Hopefully, this profile will help us narrow our suspect list and bring us one step closer to catching the killer. I must stay diligent and thorough in our investigation to ensure justice is served.

"Aurora. There you are. I was looking for you." Sam says. "I was finally able to analyze the purple roses."

"Great. Break it down for me," I tell her.

"First, I wasn't able to find any fingerprints. Secondly, the chemical composition of the petals is unlike any other flower I've encountered before." She pauses, looking intrigued. "It's as if these roses were genetically modified in some way," Sam concludes, her eyes widening with curiosity.

"So whomever sent those roses created them?" I asked her.

Sam nods. "That's my theory. And whoever did it went to great lengths to keep their identity hidden." I can't help but feel a sense of unease at the thought of someone going to such extremes just to send a message.

"That's not all, is it?" I questioned. She wouldn't have come all the way up here just to tell me that.

Sam hesitates before continuing, "There's one more thing. The scent of these roses is oddly familiar, almost nostalgic in a way. But not like roses. It's hard to describe, but it's definitely a scent I've encountered before. " As she speaks, a shiver runs down my spine, adding to the mystery surrounding the enigmatic bouquet. Bring the roses close. I take a deep sniff. The scent triggers a distant memory, but I can't quite place it. Sam watches me closely, waiting for my reaction.

"Your right. It is familiar. I also cannot place it." I comment.

"I will keep looking into it. I will find something." She assures me. Speeding off to do what she does best. As she walks away, I can't shake the feeling that the answer is just out of reach, waiting to be uncovered.

I make a mental note to keep an eye out for any clues that might lead me to the source of that haunting scent.

The weight of the case settled heavily on my shoulders as I settled into my cluttered office. Today was the day I would face the daunting task of creating a profile for the serial killer who had been terrorizing their city. Only the rhythmic tapping of my fingers against the weathered oak desk could break the eerie silence in the air, filled with anticipation and dread.

"Alright, Aurora," I muttered, my voice barely a whisper. "Let's get this done."

A single case file, crime scene photos, and victim reports lay before me, a grim testament to the killer's ruthless spree. I took a deep breath, my gaze sweeping over the evidence. This profile was not just another assignment; it was a chance to give voice to the victims, understand their tormentors' minds, and bring whoever to justice.

"Patterns, behaviors, motivations," I murmured, eyes scanning the documents. "Every detail matters."

With meticulous precision, I began compiling the evidence, my sharp mind dissecting each piece of information. The killer's victims were all young women; their lives were tragically cut short in a flurry of violence. The crime scenes were chaotic, a gruesome tapestry of blood and rage. Yet, within the chaos, there were subtle patterns emerging whispers of the killer's twisted psyche. The killer likely seeks to exert power and control over their victims, fulfilling a deep-seated need for dominance. The violent and sadistic nature of the crimes suggests a strong sexual component to the killings especially since his victims were found naked. The specific victims profile and ritualistic elements point towards an obsession and the fulfillment of a twisted fantasy. The targeting of young women could indicate underlying misogynistic beliefs and a desire to punish or degrade them.

Hours I was melted away as I immersed myself in the investigation. The killer's modus operandi, his weapon of choice, the locations he targeted—each clue added another brushstroke to the portrait I was creating. The killer's modus operandi, targeting plus-size young women, possibly reflecting a specific fantasy or obsession. The hunting ground is unknown, but likely familiar territory where the killer can easily stalk and abduct victims. The method of killing is brutal and violent, involving close-quarters combat and possibly a bladed weapon. Judging by these photos the killer most likely engages in post-mortem mutilation, potentially as a form of sexual gratification or a ritualistic act. Leaves paw prints behind, possibly as a form of psychological manipulation or a way to taunt the authorities. The room grew dark as the sun dipped below the horizon, casting long shadows across the walls. Nevertheless, I persisted in my efforts to comprehend the darkness that lay within the killer's mind.

Finally, as the first rays of dawn peeked through the blinds, I leaned back in my chair, my eyes heavy with exhaustion. The profile was as complete as it could be—a chilling glimpse into the twisted mind of a predator. It was a starting point, a roadmap for their investigation.

"We're coming for you," I whispered, my voice filled with quiet resolve. "We won't rest until you're brought to justice." With a deep breath, I gathered my notes and prepared to present our findings to the team. The hunt for the killer was far from over, but we were one step closer to unraveling the mystery and bringing closure to the victims' families. I walked into the conference room. The team's eyes met mine, filled with determination and a shared sense of purpose. As I began to lay out the details of our investigation, I knew that together, we would stop at nothing to catch the perpetrator and bring them to justice.

"Here is what I have compiled," I began, my voice steady despite the exhaustion that clung to me. "Our UNSUB," I continued, using the acronym for "unknown subject," "appears to have a specific type. So far, all of his victims have been young women between the ages of eighteen and twenty-five. They are all similar in height and build, with long, dark crimson or copper-colored hair and hazel eyes."

I paused, allowing the weight of this detail to sink in. The room fell silent as my colleagues absorbed this information. The specificity of the killer's preferences sent a chill down my spine. It spoke to a level of premeditation and calculation that was both disturbing and fascinating.

Something in me froze. I have a chilling feeling as I listen to my own voice paint a vivid picture of my own appearance. Is it a coincidence? Or is the killer deliberately targeting individuals who resemble me? The thought sent shivers down my spine, making me question everything I thought I knew about the case.

"This is not random," I emphasized continuing. "The killer is choosing his victims deliberately, based on a particular set of criteria. This could be a manifestation of a deep-seated fantasy or a twisted form of obsession."

"Do we know what the killer looks like?" An officer asks.

"As of now no. The killer's physical characteristics and traits remain elusive, making identification challenging. The crime scenes does suggest the killer possesses above-average strength and agility, given the victims' size and the violence of the attacks." I continued. "A past trauma or rejection involving a woman who resembled the victims may have served as the catalyst for the killer's actions, which may have resulted in a distorted sense of vengeance or a desire to exert control over those who remind them of their past suffering."

I displayed a series of photographs on the projector screen, each a portrait of a vibrant young woman whose life had been cut short. Their faces, frozen in time, were a haunting reminder of the stakes involved in our investigation.

"These women," I said, thick with emotion, "were daughters, sisters, and friends. They had dreams, aspirations, and futures. "A monster who preys on the defenseless stole their lives from them."

I could see the anger and sorrow in the eyes of my colleagues. We were all deeply affected by the tragedy that had befallen these young women. It was a shared grief that fueled our determination to catch the killer and bring him to justice.

"Detective McCoy." Officer Jones interrupts. "Never mind."

"No, go ahead," I told her. I might not like her but we could use all the clues possible.

She hesitated before finally speaking up. "It's just that I noticed something. Um. It's probably nothing, but I thought I should say something."

"There are no dumb questions or anything," I assured her. "What did you notice?" I prompted, eager to hear any potential leads in the case.

"You favor the victims." She finally said, her voice barely above a whisper. I felt a chill run down my spine as I realized the implications of her observation. I quickly turned around to take another look at the victims. Hair color, check. Eye color. Kind of. Body type, check. Age, different. My mind raced as I tried to make sense of her observation. They only favor me because they are all plus-size black women with red hair, which in itself is a bit weird. I haven't seen many women with that hair color before. Could the killer have dyed their hair? To what? To match mine. The thought sent shivers down my spine as I considered the possibility that the killer was trying to mimic me. Was this some twisted game they were playing, or was there a deeper connection between us that I hadn't yet realized? The idea made my blood run cold as I realized the danger I might be in.

Could this be the pattern in the victims that I hadn't noticed before? "Thank you for bringing this to my attention. You are not wrong. Other than them being younger than me, there are some similarities. Not sure if there is enough to go off." I said, trying to sound calm despite the unease creeping in. I needed to dig deeper into this new information and see if there was a connection that could help us solve the case. Officer Jones statement hung in the air, a challenge to our collective expertise.

"Detective McCoy, is there a possibility that we have missed this crucial detail in our investigation?" Officer Lawrence asked. "If so, then both you and Officer Jones would need to be careful since you both have similar physical features to the victims."

"I am unsure. This revelation could be a mere coincidence," I replied, my mind racing with possibilities. "I will have someone else reexamine the evidence and consider all angles to ensure we don't overlook any crucial information. Let's continue."

As I dove deeper into the profile, I could see its impact on my colleagues. Their expressions hardened, a mixture of disgust and determination clouding their features. They understood the gravity of the situation and the urgency of our task.

"This is a complex individual," I continued, "driven by a deep-seated rage and a need for control. He is meticulous in his planning, leaving few clues behind. But there are patterns and vulnerabilities we can exploit. But worse, he is a werewolf. This adds a supernatural element. Which is why you are all here. Each one of you are familiar with the supernatural and hold abilities of your own. Considering the brutality and animalistic nature of the attacks, we can't rule out anything at this point, especially considering the interest of the FBI in this case."

A murmur of surprise rippled through the room at the mention of the FBI's involvement. All eyes turned to the back of the room, where FBI Special Agent Caleb Nichols sat, his expression unreadable.

"Agent Nichols," I addressed him directly, "would you care to elaborate on the Bureau's interest in this case?"

Caleb leaned forward, his gaze sweeping across the room, before settling back on me. "We have reason to believe that this case may be connected to a larger investigation. The details are classified at this time, but rest assured, we are committed to working with you to bring this killer to justice. I am also here on behalf of the Night Howl."

His words hung in the air, heavy with unspoken implications. The tension in the room thickened as we all grappled with the new information. This case was far more complex than we had initially realized, and the stakes were higher than ever before.

"That's right. Agent Nichols is the Alpha of the Night Howl Wolf Pack." I reminded. Agent Nichols' revelation about being from the Night Howl Wolf Pack added another intrigue to the investigation. Clearly, we were dealing with a formidable opponent, and our team would need to be extra vigilant moving forward. "Any questions? No, good. You are all dismissed."

As everyone else left the room, I continued to analyze the victims, a sense of urgency washed over me, knowing that time was of the essence in catching the perpetrator before another victim fell prey to their sinister plan. Now that i have new information, I need to find out if there are any relations with me. I need to get back to researching the victims with a new perspective.

'Who could be doing this?" I whispered into the empty room. No one came to mind. I might butt heads with people, but no one has expressed such violence to me. "Ok think. Something out of the ordinary. What has been happening around me that is different? The fucking purple roses. They have been showing up on my desk, but I am not sure how they got there."

Could someone be trying to send me a message through these mysterious purple roses? I need to be extra cautious and vigilant moving forward. It's possible that the purple roses are a subtle warning or threat, indicating that someone is watching my every move. I need to stay alert and keep track of any other unusual occurrences that may be happening around me. Perhaps I should consider speaking to someone about this unsettling situation if it gets worse.

Chapter 6

Caleb

The sharp ring rang out through the tense silence of the precinct, and we all looked up as the 10-65 code flashed on the screen, sending a jolt of adrenaline through my veins. Missing person. My gut clenched, the dispatcher's voice confirming our worst fears. Another young woman had vanished; she would be the eighth in as many weeks to have been reported missing. The sense of urgency in the room was palpable as we quickly mobilized to begin the search, knowing that time was of the essence in cases like these. The pattern was becoming alarmingly clear, and we were determined to do everything in our power to bring this latest victim home safely.

I knew she felt it too—the unspoken connection that simmered beneath our professional interactions. The tension between us was electric, a mix of unresolved feelings and the shared burden of our past.

But right now, there is no time for personal distractions. Lives were at stake, and we were the only ones who could stop this predator.

I crossed the room, my footsteps echoing in the otherwise empty precinct. Aurora looked up, her eyes meeting mine with curiosity and wariness. "Caleb." She acknowledged her voice, a husky whisper that sent a shiver down my spine. She didn't even realize she used my name.

"10-65," I said, the words heavy with the weight of the situation. "Another one."

Her face hardened, and the playful spark in her eyes was replaced by a steely resolve. "Damn it." She muttered, pushing back her chair and rising to her feet. "We need to move fast."

I nodded, my wolf resonating with urgency. This was our chance to protect the innocent, and to finally bring justice to those who preyed on the vulnerable. Together, we would hunt this monster down, no matter the cost.

As we stepped out of the precinct, the city lights casting long shadows across the rain-slicked streets, I couldn't help but feel a sense of foreboding. This case was different and darker, and it would test us both in ways we had never imagined. But with Aurora by my side, I knew we could face any challenge or threat.

"Agent Nichols. Let's go." Aurora calls out, snapping me out of my thoughts and back into action.

We raced to the scene, adrenaline pumping through my veins. According to the dispatch, the missing woman was Denise Jones. A 24-year-old college student went missing after leaving her night class at the university. Her roommate reported her missing. As we pulled up to Cleveland State University, I couldn't help but glance at Aurora. This is her old school. Her face was a mix of fright and concern.

"Detective McCoy. Is everything alright?" I asked her.

Aurora took a deep breath before responding, "Yeah, it brings back memories." I could tell this case was hitting close to home for her.

"You went to this university, correct?" I inquired.

"Yes, back when I wanted to be a psychologist. Just a young twenty-four year old..." She replied. Stopping mid-sentence. "Let's go."

We got out of the car and walked to the last place Denise was seen. Between the library and parking lot A. As we approached the spot, Aurora's expression hardened, eyes scanning the area for clues. Her memories of her time at the university were probably flooding back, adding a personal urgency to our investigation.

As we searched for evidence, I noticed Aurora's hands were shaking slightly. She is not the type to be affected this badly by a case. Something has to be wrong. I decided to keep a close eye on Aurora, knowing there was more to her reaction than she let on. Her behavior was out of character, and I needed to figure out what was truly bothering her before we could progress in our investigation.

Searching the area where Denise went missing was turning out to be harder than I originally thought. Using my enhanced senses, I took a deep breath. The scent of decay lingered in the air, confirming my suspicions that we were not looking for a missing person. There are too many scents passing through here. None of which I could place.

There was no evidence. The lack of physical evidence was frustrating. Not even a piece of hair was found. Someone cleaned up the area Denise was taken from. This level of meticulous cleanup indicated that whoever was responsible for Denise's disappearance was thorough and possibly had experience covering their tracks. It was clear that we were dealing with a skilled and calculated individual.

"Detective McCoy. We should consider sending in a forensic team to see if they can uncover any hidden evidence we may have missed." I suggested breaking the silence that had settled between us. "It's our best shot at finding any leads in this case."

"Agreed. I will call it in." She nodded and began making the call. Just then, my phone went off. I received a message from Jason; he was in Denise's dorm room speaking to her roommate.

"You need to see this." He texted.

"Be there in 5 minutes," I replied.

"Jason has something to show us," I informed Aurora after she finished her call.

"Let's head over there right away," Aurora suggested a sense of urgency in her voice. We quickly gathered our things and went to Denise's dorm room to meet Jason and see what he had discovered. Upon arriving, we found Jason looking anxious, something I couldn't quite put my finger on. He led us to Denise's room, where we found a mysterious note and purple roses that read, "Roses are purple, and violets are blue, but something sinister is coming for you." Jason explained that he found it under Denise's pillow, and we all exchanged worried glances as we tried to make sense of the cryptic message. Aurora went pale.

"Detective McCoy. Detective McCoy. Aurora." I repeated her name, trying to snap her out of her trance.

She finally looked up, her eyes wide with fear. "I think I know what this means." She whispered, sending a chill down my spine. Aurora's revelation left us all on edge, wondering what she had uncovered. The sense of impending danger grew stronger as we realized the gravity of the situation.

"We need to get back to the office now." Aurora commended.

"Jason, handle this," I instructed, knowing we needed to act quickly before it was too late. We rushed back to the office with a sense of urgency to unravel the mystery that lay before us.

"Talk to me, Aurora," I told her. She just kept looking straight ahead and mumbling to herself. I could see the fear in her eyes, making my heart race. As we entered the office, I knew whatever Aurora had discovered was more dangerous than we imagined.

She called for everyone on the case to meet in the conference room and then left. The tension in the room was palpable as we all gathered, waiting for Aurora to return and reveal what she had found. The clock was ticking, and we knew time was of the essence in solving this mystery before it was too late.

She walked back, holding a vase of dying purple flowers. My mind raced, connecting the dots. The victims were all similar in age and appearance and may have ties to the supernatural community. A point I was looking into secretly. A chilling pattern was emerging, with my guts in knots, and I couldn't figure out why. And now it hit me like a ton of bricks. My gaze drifted towards Aurora; her brow furrowed in concentration as she studied the flowers.

"Since about a month ago, I noticed that someone has been sending me purple roses. I don't know how long this has been happening. I don't know who is doing it. I found them on my desk, and at first I was going to throw them out. The first time I noticed them, I asked Director Martinez to look into it."

"And I have been. Unfortunately, I was not able to find anything. The only flower shop that sells purple flowers do not have purple roses and have not sold any purple flowers in the last couple of months. The sender seems to be very discreet and careful not to leave any trace behind. It's unsettling to think that someone has been able to access my office without being noticed." Uncle comments.

"A few days ago, these were found on my desk. I took them to Sam to have them analyzed. Sam was able to determine that someone is artificially making these purple roses." Aurora spoke, her voice barely above a whisper. "Each time, a simple note came with them. This one says: "Roses are purple. Violets are blue. Your time is up. I'm coming for you. Then yesterday, Officer Jenny Jones pointed out that I favor the victims."

"Apparently, the purple rose is a symbol of admiration and enchantment." Aurora continued, her eyes meeting Director Martinez's with dismay and fear. "I saw the similarities, but they weren't big. It wasn't until today that I realized I might be connected to the case. We found purple roses with a note saying, "Roses are purple, and violets are blue, but something sinister is coming for you at Denise dorm room."

Director Martinez's expression darkened as he processed the information, his mind obviously racing with the implications of Aurora's revelation. How could she keep this to herself? Weeks. She has known me for weeks that someone was sending her creep messages.

"I'm sorry, uncle. I didn't think it was relevant until now." Aurora said, her voice tinged with regret. "I didn't want to cause unnecessary panic, but I see now that it was a mistake." Director Martinez nodded slowly, his eyes narrowing as he contemplated the potential danger that Aurora's connection to the case could bring.

"Is this why you have been feeling out of sorts?" I questioned.

"Yes, I couldn't shake the feeling that something was wrong, but I didn't know why." My inner wolf replied. **"I didn't know it involved our mate."**

"What if the killer is targeting those who look like me?" My head snapped up at her remark. The realization sent a shiver down my spine, knowing that she may be the next victim in this deadly game. "I have been studying the victim's profiles, and there is something there. I just cannot place what. I will start at square one again."

"As of today, you are on desk duty." Director Martinez says. Aurora nodded, looking frustrated at being sidelined but knowing it was for her safety. She would have to find a way to continue the investigation behind a desk.

"I will find the link," Aurora promised, determination shining in her eyes. Despite being confined to desk duty, she would not give up until she cracked the case and stopped the killer.

"Everyone, leave the room but Aurora, Agent Caleb, and Agent Jason." Director Martinez's voice cut through the tension in the room, signaling that a new development was about to unfold. Aurora exchanged a knowing glance with her colleagues, ready to dive deeper into the investigation with their help. "Some things are just not for everyone to hear."

"Uncle?" Aurora called.

"Agent Caleb, do you know anyone in your pack that overly liked Aurora or has any reason to harm her?" Director Martinez's question hung in the air, causing a chill to run down my spine. As the room fell silent, all eyes turned to Agent Caleb, who hesitated before responding.

"I'm not sure." I finally admitted it; my expression was troubled. The tension in the room thickened as everyone waited for my answer, realizing that this new lead could be crucial to finally catching the killer. "But I can promise you, I will find out. Rest assured; I will do everything I can to get to the bottom of this." I added firmly, determined to uncover the truth no matter what it took. The weight of Aurora's gaze lingered on me, a silent reminder of the urgency and importance of the task. I will not allow anyone to harm her. I could see the fear in Aurora's eyes, and I knew I had to act quickly to protect her. As I left the room, a sense of determination washed over me, fueling my resolve to bring justice to those responsible for the crimes.

I quickly grabbed my phone and sent out an encrypted email to my father containing the current dates of when the known victims went missing. Hopefully, he can find something out and soon.

Chapter 7

Aurora

The hair on the back of my neck prickled with an unwelcome sensation. An all new sensation. A cold shiver danced down my spine, though the summer heat hung heavy in the air. My instincts were on high alert, warning me of potential danger lurking in the darkness. My sealed powers are tingling beneath the surface. The feeling of being watched intensified, causing my heart to race with unease. I quickened my pace to the car, my eyes darting from shadow to shadow as I made my way home from the precinct. Caleb is right beside me. No one would let me go home alone. As we reached the car's safety, I couldn't shake the feeling that something was still watching us from the shadows. I quickly unlocked the car and jumped inside, my heart racing with fear.

If only I wasn't sealed. I could have easily used my powers to sense any danger lurking nearby. At most I can project a shield or blind them. But for now, all I could do was rely on Caleb's protection and hope that whatever was watching us would not follow.

Once inside the car, I sighed in relief and turned to Caleb, grateful for his presence. As we drove away, the streetlights illuminated our path, leaving the darkness and its unseen threats behind. I couldn't help but feel a sense of unease creeping up my spine, wondering if we were indeed out of danger. Caleb must have sensed my uneasiness as he reached over and squeezed my hand reassuringly. The familiar sound of the engine humming and the warmth of the car enveloped me, easing my tension slightly.

Needing to distract myself, I turned to look at Caleb. He's closeness—a comforting warmth against the chilling fear—stirred a different awareness within me. The scent of his cologne, a blend of musk and something subtly sweet, filled my senses, drawing me to him in a way I hadn't allowed myself to acknowledge lately. The gentle brush of his arm against mine sent a shiver down my spine, and I longed for his touch, strength, and unwavering support.

His touch made me remember a distant past. When we were happy, If I am being honest, leaving him was my biggest regret. I found myself lost in memories of our shared laughter and stolen kisses—the thrill of forbidden nights under the full moon. The pain of our separation—the raw ache of my betrayal—felt like a distant echo, momentarily drowned out by the resurgence of dormant desires.

The case at hand—the gruesome murders that haunted my dreams—seemed to fade into the background as I focused on the man beside me. His presence was a potent distraction, a dangerous temptation that threatened to derail my focus and compromise my judgment. As I struggled with conflicting emotions, I couldn't deny the undeniable chemistry that still existed between us. The familiar warmth of his presence enveloped me, making me question if maybe there was still a chance for us to rekindle what we once had.

I knew I was playing with fire, but the allure of the familiar was too strong to resist. In that moment, I allowed myself to be vulnerable, to let down my guard, and to embrace the forbidden desire that threatened to consume us both. If Caleb was to look at me, my eyes would show a mixture of longing and uncertainty.

A pang of loneliness struck me, a reminder of the nights I spent tossing and turning, missing the comfort of his presence beside me. I miss this. Caleb by my side. I miss him. I can admit to it now. I can't deny that I still long for him, despite trying to convince myself otherwise. The ache in my heart grows stronger each day, a silent plea for his return.

As we continued on our journey, my mind was going crazy. I need to find the link between the victims and me. Caleb's comforting touch provided some solace, but the mystery still lingered in my mind. I couldn't shake the feeling that something connected me to the victims, and I was determined to uncover the truth.

"Thank you." I finally managed to say something.

Caleb gave me a small smile, his eyes filled with understanding. "We'll figure this out together." He replied softly, his grip on my hand tightening slightly.

It took a little to no time to get to my penthouse. As I stepped inside, the weight of the situation settled in, and I knew that unraveling this mystery would be no easy task. I needed a shower first because I felt dirty. I quickly went to the bathroom, letting the hot water wash away the day's events. As I scrubbed away the grime, my mind raced with thoughts of what could be lurking beneath the surface of this case. I started putting the pieces together.

It had started with small things—purple roses with an anonymous note. At first, I dismissed them as coincidences—the paranoid ramblings of an overworked detective. As the weeks passed, with no further changes, I left it alone. But now, with a murder case on my hands and the pieces starting to fit together, I couldn't ignore the feeling that those small details were connected to something much bigger.

Another coincidence is that Officer Jenny Jones looks like me too. How old is she again? I need to look into it. Could she be part of this? The resemblance between Officer Jenny Jones and myself is uncanny, and her involvement in the case cannot be overlooked. I must investigate further to determine if she is connected to the mysterious pieces falling into place.

As I dried off and dressed, I knew it was time to delve deeper into this mystery and follow the trail wherever it may lead. Denise went missing from my old university. She was 24 years old at the time. When I first started at CSU, I was twenty-four years old. Shit. Caleb and I would often take the route between the library and parking lot A since my psychology classes were next to there when he picked me up.

Wait, what about Ashley? We found her at the old mill. She'd just turned twenty-three. The last time I was at the old mill, I was with Caleb. I'd just turned twenty-three, and we went there to act like a couple of kids. Oh, no. What about the other victims? Do they have anything in relation to me? To Caleb?

Ok, slow down. Think Aurora. How is this connected? Could it be a coincidence that all the victims were around the same age as when Caleb and I used to date? So far, two victims lined up with when I was dating Caleb. Is this the connection I'm missing?

"Caleb," I called as I walked into my living room.

"In the kitchen." He called back. I found Caleb sitting at the table, sipping coffee and flipping through a file. "I need your help with something," I said, my voice filled with urgency.

Caleb looked up, concern evident in his eyes. "What's going on?" he asked, setting the file aside. I took a deep breath, knowing that with Caleb's help, we could uncover the truth behind the mysterious pieces falling into place.

"We need to work together and stay one step ahead of the killer." Caleb agreed, his expression grim. "Let's run through the victims. Let's start with the first known victim." I began, my mind already racing through the details of the case, the faces of the victims flashing before my eyes. "Her name was Emily Davis. She was nineteen years old when she was killed."

"According to her file, she was last seen at Luke Easter Park skating rink. Zelma Watson-George Recreation Center." Caleb continued.

"You throw me a surprise birthday party. I think I just turned nineteen." I added. "Next is..."

"Mia Collins." Caleb supplied, his voice barely above a whisper. "She was twenty, and she was found at the botanical gardens." Caleb's words sent a chill down my spine as memories of our past outings flooded my mind. The connection between the victims and our personal history was becoming increasingly unsettling.

"We used to go there all the time. It is one of my favorite places to go. The last time we went there together was for my twentieth birthday. They had the butterfly exhibit." I added.

"The third victim is Jordan Rivers. She was twenty-one and disappeared from Dave and Busters." Caleb continued.

"Dave and Busters was where we celebrated our second anniversary. I was twenty-one at the time." I added, feeling a sense of dread creeping in. The realization that all three victims had ties to places significant in our relationship made me question everything.

"When did we start dating?" I asked.

"Since you were eighteen." He replied with a small smile. I remember the day we met at Randal Park Mall. It was one of the best days of my life.

"And when did we break up?" I asked.

"When you were... Shit." He stated. Realizing the reason behind my questioning. "You were twenty-eight. You don't think?"

"And, how old am I now?" I asked. Ignoring his question.

"You will be thirty in a few days. The killer is killing by your age." He spoked.

"Exactly," I said, my heart pounding as the pieces started to come together. "We need to act fast before it's too late. There will at least be two more victims."

"Why at least two?" He questioned.

"Because I think I will be the thirtieth one," I said darkly. "Probably on my thirtieth birthday. I think the killer was going off the age when I started dating you."

"We know of four, maybe five, victims. If we are truly going by your age when we were dating, we are missing several bodies." The thought of potentially more victims out there, possibly linked to our past, sent a chill down my spine. It was clear that the investigation was far from over, and the unsettling connection between the victims and our personal history only deepened the mystery.

As we delved deeper into the case, it became apparent that a sinister pattern was emerging, one that seemed to be targeting us specifically. The fear of what we might uncover next weighed heavily on my mind as we continued to piece together the puzzle.

Each victim we know about has disappeared at some place related to us. As we connected the dots, it became increasingly evident that we were not just bystanders in this investigation but potentially critical players in unraveling the truth behind these disappearances. Realizing that our safety could be at risk added a sense of urgency to our pursuit of answers. The more we delved into the details, the more it seemed someone was trying to send us a message. The chilling thought that we were being watched only fueled our determination to get to the bottom of this mystery before it was too late.

"Aurora. I will not let that anything happen to you." Caleb declared, determination shining in his eyes. "We will catch this killer."

"We need to figure out who the killer is targeting next and stop them before it's too late," I urged. "We can't let anyone else become a victim." The urgency in my voice matched the fear in my heart as we raced against time to prevent more tragedy.

"Going off of what we know and the age of the victims we know about, the next victim will be either twenty-five and disappear from Cedar Point, or twenty-six and disappear from the Cavs game, twenty-seven and disappear from Cleveland Metroparks Zoo, or twenty-eight and disappear from Pier W. This all depends on what age the killer is currently at." I note.

"I will inform the others what we found." Caleb cuts in. Not allowing me to finish what I was saying. But he was right. I left him. I couldn't help but feel a pang of guilt as Caleb mentioned the place where I had rejected his proposal. I knew I had hurt him deeply, and the thought of him bringing it up amid a severe investigation made me feel even worse.

As we parted ways, he went to make the call, and I needed to be alone. We didn't have time for my emotions. We needed to act quickly to prevent another tragedy, especially since the message was a personal vendetta against us. The situation's urgency weighed heavily on our shoulders as we prepared to uncover the truth behind these disturbing events.

Chapter 8

Caleb

The weight of leadership pressed heavily on my shoulders, a burden I had carried since I was named Alpha. The pack looked to me for guidance, protection, and strength. And now, as my world collided with Aurora's once again, my heart ached with a familiar conflict—a battle between duty and desire.

Caught between my responsibilities to my pack and the undeniable pull towards Aurora and wanting to protect her, I knew that I had to make a choice that would impact my own future and the fate of those who depended on me. The stakes were higher than ever, and I could feel the tension mounting as I struggled to balance loyalty and love.

I watched her from across the dimly lit room, her fiery hair a beacon in my haze. She was deep in thought. After we found out, I am sure her mind is running a mile a minute. The years had been kind to her, softening her features while accentuating her natural beauty. There was a fire in her eyes that had never dimmed, a fierce determination that had always drawn me to her.

But there was also a distance—a wall she had erected between them after their painful breakup. She left me. I couldn't blame her for wanting to protect herself, but I couldn't help but hope that maybe, just maybe, we could find our way back to each other.

Despite everything, I still believed in our love. I know why she made her choice. I knew I had hurt her and had made choices that prioritized my pack over our passion. The guilt gnawed at me, a constant reminder of my failures.

Yet, I couldn't deny the thrill that coursed through me at the sight of her. The old feelings, dormant but never truly extinguished, stirred within me. I longed to reach out, to bridge the gap that separated us, but I knew it wouldn't be easy.

Aurora's investigation into the ritualistic murders had brought us back together; our paths were intertwined once more. I couldn't help but admire her tenacity and unwavering pursuit of justice. But her involvement in the case also filled me with dread.

Someone is after her, and someone may be from my pack.

The secrets of my pack and the delicate balance of power within the werewolf community were at stake. I knew that Aurora, with her relentless curiosity and sharp mind, would uncover truths that could shatter the fragile peace I had worked so hard to maintain.

I knew I had to tread carefully, balancing my loyalty to my pack with my desire to help Aurora. I had to protect my people but couldn't bear to see Aurora in danger. The conflict tore at me, a constant struggle between my head and heart.

I knew that I couldn't stay away. I had to be by Aurora's side, even if it meant risking everything. I rose from my seat, my resolve hardening. I would face this challenge head-on, just as I had faced countless others before. I was the Alpha, after all, and I wouldn't let anything, or anyone stand in the way of protecting those he cared about. I am going to protect Aurora.

But first, I need to talk to my father. See if he found any clues. I needed to gather as much information as possible before confronting whatever threat loomed ahead.

Hopping into my car, I headed for the cove. The salty sea air filled my lungs as I approached the familiar spot where my father often went to think. As I stepped out of the car, I could feel the weight of responsibility settling on my shoulders. Walking down the winding pathway, I spotted my father. He was sitting on a weathered bench, staring out at the crashing waves with a contemplative expression. I took a deep breath and prepared myself for the conversation that would hopefully provide the answers I needed to protect Aurora.

"Father." I called out to him.

He turned to me, his eyes reflecting both surprise and concern. Without saying a word, I knew that this conversation would be difficult, but necessary for the safety of our community.

"What brings you here?" He questioned me.

"Have you found out anything?" I replied with a question.

"There are a few members who were missing during the time frames you gave me." He resopnsed. Pulling out a piece of paper. "I am only doing this to protect the pack. Why are you?"

"What kind of question is that? I am trying to protect the pack also." I replied.

"She is not part of the pack." He commented.

"Father, there is a killer going around, and he is targeting young women. We need to find out who it is before it's too late." I explained, hoping to convince him of the urgency of the situation. He hands me the piece of paper. The paper contained names and dates for which each person was unaccountable. Olivia Smith, Emma Johnson, Sophia Brown, Noah Davis, Liam Wilson, Oliver Miller, Elijah Taylor, and Luke Miller. Eight people. I knew each one of them. "Thank you, Father. This helps. I will start investigating right away." I assured him before heading out to gather more information on the potential killer. The list of names was a starting point, but I knew there was much more work to be done to protect the young women in our community.

Where do I start first? I decided to start at the drawing board. Jumping into my car, I headed back to the percinct. I needed to organize the information I had and prioritize my next steps in the investigation. As I drove, my mind raced with possibilities and strategies to uncover the truth behind these mysterious disappearances.

As I walked into the precinct, I knew that my first task would be to review all the evidence we had gathered so far and see if any patterns or connections emerged. I also needed to coordinate with the rest of the team to ensure that we were all on the same page and working towards a common goal. Let's put this data together.

Sophia Brown, Elijah Taylor, and Noah Davis were unaccountable for two of the missing victims.

Liam Wilson, Olivia Smith, and Oliver Miller were unaccountable for three of the missing victims.

Emma Johnson and Luke Miller were unaccountable for four of the missing victims.

If I rule out Sophia Brown, Elijah Taylor, and Noah Davis, that leaves five possible suspects. By eliminating Liam Wilson, Olivia Smith, and Oliver Miller as well, we can narrow down the list of suspects to three individuals. Further investigation into Emma Johnson may reveal more information about her potential involvement in the case. Luke and Oliver have been on vacation, visiting family, for the past month. It is slightly odd that Oliver came back to the pack during his vacation. But it is not out of the ordinary; some of the members of the pack prefer the pack.

Ok. Slow down. Let's find out what Ms. Emma Johnson is doing. With my laptop in hand, I swiftly enter Emma's name and information into the FBI database. As I hit enter, I wait anxiously for the results to come up on the screen. If Emma Johnson has any criminal history or connections to the case, this search could be a major breakthrough in solving it.

The first thing I saw was a picture of Emma. This is not good; she favors Aurora. Her hair color is a bit off, but she could pass as Aurora's sister. According to the FBI database, Emma has been missing for the past two weeks. She was reported to be missing by her boyfriend, Aaron Taylor. Aaron, being a human, decided to go to the local police station to report her as missing. She was last seen at Playhouse Square. Aaron mentioned that she went to use the bathroom and never returned. Wait, how old was Emma when she went missing? Based on the database records, her age was recorded as twenty-two.

Think, Caleb. Aurora and I went to see the Loin King at Playhouse Square once. How old was Aurora then? Twenty-two? It's quite likely that Emma is more of a victim than a suspect. .

Shit. This puts me back at square one on suspects. It seems I need to shift my focus. Other than Emma, Luke was unaccountable the most. It's time to verify his claims of being out of town. We can start by cross-checking his travel records and any credit card transactions made during that period.

Also, I shouldn't completely rule out Oliver just yet. While his return during vacation might be explainable, it still raises suspicion. Let's see if I can find any additional information about his whereabouts during his time away and his reason for coming back. First, let's connect the Financial Crimes Section. They have the authority and resources to track credit card information as part of investigations.

Right as I was finishing up an email to track the Miller brothers credit card history to the Financial Crimes Section, I got a text from Aurora. She mentions that Director Martinez has summoned us in.

Chapter 9

Aurora

What am I going to do? I took a deep breath, reminding myself to stay focused and rational in the face of adversity. It was crucial to keep a clear mind. I knew that allowing my emotions to take over would only hinder our progress. With determination, I pushed aside my personal turmoil and focused on the task at hand, knowing that time was of the essence.

With a knock on the door, Caleb arrived at my place in record time. As I glanced at the camera, there he was, standing outside with a determined expression on his face. I knew we were in this together, ready to face whatever challenges came our way.

As I opened the door, the air crackled with unspoken words. I saw the pain and longing reflected in Caleb's eyes, a mirror to my heart's turmoil. We'd danced around each other for too long, pretending that the past hadn't carved its initials into our souls. But as we stood there in silence, the weight of our unspoken emotions hung heavy between us, begging to be acknowledged. It was time to confront the truth we had avoided for far too long.

In that instant, the lines between detective and FBI agent, between ex-lovers and potential allies, blurred. All I could see was the man I had once loved—the man who still held a piece of me captive.

His hand reached out, tentative, and I met it halfway. The warmth of his touch was a familiar solace, a reminder of happier times. Our eyes met, and a silent conversation passed between us, a bridge over the years of hurt and misunderstanding.

I closed the distance; the pull between us was too strong to resist. My lips found Caleb's—a gentle pressure, then a deepening surrender. It wasn't just a kiss but a confession, a reunion, a promise whispered against his mouth.

When we finally broke apart, the air felt charged and electric. The weight of the world hadn't disappeared, not entirely. However, for a brief moment, there had only been the two of us—two souls intertwined and connected by a love that would not let go.

I knew the challenges ahead would be challenging, but I wouldn't. There were still secrets to uncover, a killer to catch, and a delicate balance between my heart and my duty. But as I looked into Caleb's eyes, I saw a glimmer of hope, a shared determination to face the darkness together.

This case may give us a second chance. Not just at love but at redemption, at healing the wounds of the past. And, together, we could finally find a way to move forward.

"I shouldn't have done that," I say after the kiss. "I know, but I'm glad you did," Caleb replies with a soft smile, his eyes reflecting the same hope and determination as mine. "We have much that needs to be said."

"Agreed. And we will. It is about time. Let's not waste any more time avoiding the inevitable. Let's face our truths and move forward together." With a nod, Caleb takes my hand, and we both step into the unknown, ready to confront our past and embrace our future.

On the way to the precinct, we share a comfortable silence, each lost in our own thoughts but finding solace in the presence of the other. As we approach the building, I feel a sense of calm determination wash over me, knowing that whatever challenges lie ahead, we will face them together as a team. We walked into the building, and everyone turned to look at us.

"Detective McCoy, Agent Caleb, my office." Uncle Javier screams. We ascend to his office, filled with a mixture of nerves and eager anticipation. I know that whatever awaits me in that room, I will handle it with the same resolve that has gotten me this far in my career. "Sit, both of you. I got your message about the new details of the case. I reviewed each case file, and I believe we are on the right track. If your assessment is accurate, it appears that we have individuals aged 19, 20, 21, 23, and 24 who are victims.

"I might have found the victim at age twenty-two. Her name is Emma Johnson. She went missing at Playhouse Square." Caleb says. "She was a member of my pack and been missing for two weeks."

"Shit. We saw the Lion King there when I was twenty-two years old." I whispered.

"That's what I figured. I wasn't sure," Caleb said.

"Damn. That is six victims so far." Uncle Javier says. "Are you sure, agent?"

"Emma Johnson fits the profile of the other victims," Caleb stated, firmly nodding his head, his expression grim.

"Uncle, there's more," I told him. "We may have found out where the bodies of the next couple of victims can be found or where they might disappear from."

"Where?" He asked. "I needed to send a team there now."

"Based on the available information and the patterns observed in previous cases, it is likely that the upcoming victims will be either twenty-five and disappear from Cedar Point, or twenty-six and disappear from the Cavs game, twenty-seven and disappear from Cleveland Metroparks Zoo, or twenty-eight and disappear from Pier W. This all depends on what age the killer is currently at." I informed him.

Uncle picked up his radio. Urgently relaying the information as a potential location for the next victim. "We need to act fast," he said, his expression grave. "I honestly don't understand. How does the killer know all this information about your dates? I need both of you to compile a list of people you gave this information to. That includes me, Aurora."

I nodded, feeling a chill run down my spine, realizing that someone close to us could be involved. Uncle Javier was right—we needed to quickly catch this killer before they struck again. Sitting down, I ransacked my brain, trying to remember every person I had shared details about my dates with. The thought of someone we trusted being behind these horrific crimes was terrifying, but we needed to stay focused and work together to solve this mystery before it was too late.

My sister helps plan most of our dates. I was never good at it, so they always helped me. Caleb, however, was the one who planned the majority of the dates. He was attentive and thoughtful, ensuring every detail was perfect. As I sifted through my memories, I realized that Caleb had access to personal information about me, including where I would be on those dates. It was a chilling thought that couldn't be ignored in our search for the truth.

There is also Uncle Javier. He didn't know about all of Caleb and my dates, but I told him about the ones I deemed necessary, especially when I was younger.

Same with dad. He probably knew less than Uncle Javier.

I don't have a lot of people I talk to about my personal life.

"Uncle Javier, here is my list. It's small. Just Estrella, Maria, and Sofía know the most. Followed by you and then Dad." I informed him. Uncle Javier nodded and looked at Caleb.

"My list is not as small as Aurora's. My parents, brothers, and some members of the pack knew. The pack does not have as much information as most. If I had to say, my beta, Jason, knows the most." Caleb added. "Also, Luke Miller, my Epsilon and driver, he took us on most of our dates."

"Speaking of Luke, where is he? Isn't he supposed to be your shadow at all times?" I asked.

"He took a vacation about a month ago," Caleb says, "I already started looking into his were abouts."

"I never like him. He was always so quiet and stared creepily." I replied.

"At you?" Uncle Javier asks.

"Not really. Just period." I commented. "He made my sense tingle. I chalked it up to him being an Epsilon. Most of the ones I met kind of act like that."

"We cannot leave any stone unturned. Luke went on vacation around the time the murders started. We have to be on the safe side." Uncle Javier says.

"I am waiting on the Financial Crimes Section to respond to my email. I asked them to track his credit card information and pull anything they could find. I already looked into his accountability for the nights of the murders and missing girls. He was unaccountable for four of them," Caleb added, a look of concern crossing his face. "I can delve deeper into his vacation plans and investigate any potential links to the murders."

"Agreed, we need to act fast before it's too late," I replied, feeling urgent.

"Let's divide and conquer. You'll look into his financial records while Aurora reaches out to the local hotels and resorts to see if he has been seen in the area. We need to gather as much evidence as possible to build a solid case against him," Uncle Javier suggested as we quickly formulated a plan to get to the bottom of this mystery. As we dispersed to investigate, the weight of the situation hung heavy in the air, fueling our determination to solve the case. Time was of the essence, and we knew every second counted in unraveling the truth behind these heinous crimes.

Chapter 10

Caleb

The revelations about the chilling connection to our past only fueled my determination. The killer was taunting us, playing a twisted game with our lives. But we wouldn't let them win.

The fact that Luke, my Epsilon, may be entangled in these horrific acts filled me with disgust. Luke has been by my side since I was a child. He was chosen to be my protector after he saved my father during the last war. Luke had always been a beacon of strength and loyalty to me, but now I couldn't shake the feeling of unease. He never said anything about Aurora. He would always just drive us to and from our dates.

Despite my doubts, I knew we had to uncover the truth in order to stop the killer before more lives were lost.

I glanced at Aurora, her expression a mirror of my own resolve. Together, we would uncover the truth, no matter how painful it was. We would find the killer and bring them to justice, not just for Aurora but for all the victims who had suffered at their hands.

"This was our fight, our battle. And we would not rest until we emerged victorious." My inner wolf says.

With a shared nod, we set off on our mission, determined to seek justice and closure for those wronged. The weight of the task ahead only fueled our determination as we embarked on the journey to find Luke and put an end to the terror he had caused.

Walking to my borrowed desk, as I was getting ready to send out a mass message to my pack, trying to find out Luke's whereabouts, I realized I needed to be secretive. This included Jason. I trust Jason with my life, but my own Epsilon might be involved. I knew that keeping this information from Jason would be difficult, but it was necessary to protect Aurora and ensure the success of our mission. I made a mental note to handle the situation cautiously and precisely, knowing that the stakes were high.

Sitting down, I pulled up the Bureau database. I needed to look up the latest intel on Luke's possible whereabouts without raising any suspicion. I quickly scanned through the database, making sure to cover my tracks and leaving no trace of my search. As I sifted through the information, I couldn't shake the feeling that time was running out and every move had to be calculated.

Not pulling anything from searching for Luke's name in the FBI database, I decided to broaden my search parameters and cross-reference on social media accounts. If he is vacationing with his family, maybe someone spotted him and took a picture. This way, I could potentially gather more recent and candid sightings of him. I knew that finding Luke was crucial, and I was determined to exhaust all possible avenues to locate him.

I felt a rush of relief when I discovered a sighting reported by a nearby town, although I knew it also meant the danger had increased. Luke happened to be in the vicinity of the old mill when this picture was taken, just two days before Ashley was found. It could be a coincidence, but I couldn't shake the possibility that Luke may have been involved.

Going through the rest of the social media accounts, I found more photos of Luke in various locations, but none provided a clear lead on his current whereabouts. However, it did indicate that he frequented the locations where the crimes occurred. He was at CSU the day before Denise went missing. There is even a picture of him at Playhouse Square the day Emma Johnson went missing. In the last photo he was in, he was downtown.

This implies that he was near the scene of multiple murders and disappearances. This information was crucial for our investigation, but it also meant we needed to act quickly and cautiously. I knew that it was of the essence to protect Aurora and apprehend Luke before he could harm anyone else.

Shaking my head, I returned to Director Martinez's office. I needed to inform him of the new development and strategize our next steps. As I walked, my mind raced with possible scenarios and outcomes, knowing that every decision we made could have serious consequences. I knocked on his door and informed him, "We have a problem, Director Martinez. Luke was seen in the vicinity, not too far from here. In the downtown area."

Director Martinez's face paled as he listened to my report.

"Agent Caleb. Let me see if I can pull anything off on my end. We need more information." Director Martinez says.

He quickly picks up his computer and begins typing. I stood by, waiting anxiously as Director Martinez worked his magic, trying to gather more intel on Luke's whereabouts. The clock was ticking, and every minute that passed felt like an eternity as we raced against time to prevent any potential disaster.

"Got you, you son of a bitch. We have a lead on Luke's location," Director Martinez declares. Director Martinez announces the relief evident in his voice. "It seems he's holed up in an abandoned warehouse on the outskirts of town."

With a renewed sense of urgency, we quickly formulated a plan to apprehend Luke before he could carry out whatever nefarious scheme he had planned.

He instructed me to gather the team and prepare for immediate action without missing a beat. Time was indeed of the essence, and we needed to act swiftly to ensure everyone's safety. With a sense of urgency, I quickly relayed the message to the team and began formulating a plan of action to address the potential threat of Luke's presence in the area. Director Martinez's decisive leadership was crucial in guiding us through this critical situation, and we all knew that our response would be essential in determining the outcome.

As we geared up and headed out, the tension in the air was palpable, but we were all focused on the task at hand. Each team member knew their role and was ready to execute it precisely to neutralize any danger. Aurora had to stay behind. She was Luke's possible target. Aurora's safety was our top priority, and we planned to protect her in any unforeseen circumstances. To say that she was pissed would be an understatement. She understood the importance of her role in staying behind, but the frustration was evident in her eyes as we left. We reassured her that we would return safely and with Luke in custody, easing some of her anger.

With Director Martinez's guidance and the team's determination, we were confident in our ability to handle whatever challenges may come our way. We maintained constant communication and coordination throughout the operation, ensuring everyone was on the same page and ready to act swiftly. Director Martinez's strategic planning and quick decision- making were instrumental in keeping us one step ahead of Luke's potential threat.

As we approached the location where Luke was last seen, our training kicked in, and we were prepared to handle whatever came our way. The primal instincts of my wolf stirred within me, sharpening my senses to a heightened level. My hearing became acute, picking up even the faintest rustle of leaves in the distance. My sense of smell intensified, allowing me to detect the subtle scent of damp earth and decaying wood, but no trace of Luke.

I shifted my senses, attuning myself to the subtle vibrations in the air, the changes in temperature, and the unseen currents that only a wolf could perceive. The world around me transformed into a tapestry of sensations, a symphony of primal cues that spoke volumes to my heightened awareness.

I had to be on high alert. Luke didn't become a protector because he was weak. He was a seasoned warrior, skilled in the art of combat and survival.

We stealthily maneuvered around the building where Luke was last spotted, our movements fluid and silent, like shadows dancing in the moonlight. The air crackled with tension, the silence pressing down on us with an almost palpable weight. Inhaling deeply, I strained to catch any scent or clue that might lead us to Luke. But there was nothing, only the sterile odor of concrete and steel.

The absence of any scent was disconcerting. Wolves leave their mark wherever they go, their unique aroma lingering in the air like an invisible signature. But here, there was no trace of Luke, no hint of his presence. It was as if he had vanished into thin air.

I signaled to my team to proceed with caution, my unease growing with each passing moment. The silence, the lack of any scent, the eerie stillness of the surroundings—all of it pointed to something being amiss. We were venturing into the unknown, and danger could be lurking around any corner. My wolf growled softly in my chest, its instincts urging me to be vigilant, to be prepared for the worst.

As we moved closer, the silence grew oppressive. The absence of any sound—even the normal hum of city life in the distance—amplified the tension in the air. My wolf's instincts screamed at me, every nerve ending tingling with a sense of impending danger.

Each team member moved with practiced grace, their movements a silent ballet of lethal efficiency. With each step, the anticipation of finally confronting Luke grew stronger, fueling our determination. The image of his face, once a symbol of trust and camaraderie, now twisted into a mask of suspicion, haunted my thoughts. We had to find him, not just for the sake of the investigation but also to understand what had driven him to such desperate actions.

Once everyone was in position, we knocked on the front door. The sound echoed through the silence, but there was no answer. We tried again, the tension mounting with each passing second. Still no response. Director Martinez gave the go-ahead, and I didn't hesitate. With a powerful kick, I splintered the front door, the wood shattering under the force of my blow. Simultaneously, I could hear Jason crashing through the back entrance.

As we entered the house, the only sound was the heavy thud of our boots on the bare floor, echoing through the empty rooms. We rushed in, guns raised, our hearts pounding in our chests. The air crackled with nervous energy, and every shadow was a potential threat. We searched every corner, every closet, and every inch of the house, but there was no sign of Luke. The realization hit us like a punch to the gut: he had fled before we arrived.

The scent of decomposing flesh filled my nostrils. The stench grew stronger as we made our way through the house, leading us to a locked basement door. With a deep breath, I kicked it open, revealing a gruesome scene that confirmed our worst fears. There were numerous bodies lying motionless on the chilly concrete floor, all around them being signs of a violent struggle.

Five women were lying still in a heap on the floor. Their lifeless eyes stared up at us, frozen in terror. It was clear that Luke was not the innocent man we once thought he was. The horror of the situation sank in as we realized the true extent of his depravity.

Director Martinez radioed for backup as we continued to scour the house for any clues that might lead us to his whereabouts. Frustration gnawed at me. Luke was one step ahead, his cunning and resourcefulness making him a formidable adversary.

Suddenly, the overhead lights flickered on, illuminating the abandoned living room. In the center of the room, a crumpled piece of paper lay on the floor, a hastily scrawled message mocking us: "Roses are purple, violets are blue, you missed me, but I'll be back for you." Beside it, a vase filled with purple roses added a chilling touch to the scene.

My heart sank. Luke was taunting us, playing a twisted game of cat and mouse. The chase was far from over. We had to regroup, strategize, and anticipate his next move before he struck again. The scent of danger hung heavy in the air, and the wolf within me snarled, eager to hunt down its prey.

Chapter 11

Aurora

The case was heating up. We now have a potential suspect. Luke. He was seen in the vicinity of the area. With a sense of urgency, the team quickly prepared themselves and made their way to Luke's location, eager to gather more information.

On the other hand, I was forced to stay behind. I analyzed the evidence collected and coordinated with other departments for additional support. I knew my role was crucial in building a solid case against Luke. As the team headed out, I focused on ensuring that all pieces of evidence were thoroughly examined, and any necessary resources were secured for the investigation. With enough evidence, I obtained a warrant for entry onto the property Luke stayed on. This allowed us to thoroughly search and gather more incriminating evidence against him.

After finishing that, I still had yet to hear any news. I decided to go home for the night. Officer John Lawson was on babysitting duties, so he came with me. I knew tonight was going to be a long night. As we drove back, I couldn't shake the unease lingering in the air. Our efforts would soon lead to a breakthrough in the case.

As I fumbled with my keys, my hand trembling, I caught a glimpse of movement in the reflection of my front door. Shrouded in darkness, a tall figure stood across the street, their gaze fixed on me. My breath hitched in my throat, and I quickly unlocked the door, slamming it shut behind me.

Leaning against the door, I struggled to catch my breath, the weight of fear pressing down on me. I was a homicide detective, for God's sake, trained to handle dangerous situations. But this was different. This was personal and insidious, slowly chipping away at my sanity.

I knew I should report it and bring it to the attention of Officer John Lawson, but a part of me hesitated. Would they believe me? Would they think I was imagining things and overreacting? And what if it made things worse and provoked the stalker to take more drastic measures?

I was trapped in a twisted game of cat and mouse, the prey of a predator who revealed my fear. Standing in the darkness of my home, I realized with chilling clarity that I was no longer just a detective investigating a case. I was the case, the target, the deadly obsession of a stalker.

I was so deep in thought that I screamed when someone knocked on my door. I cried so loudly that my own voice startled me. I hesitated to answer the door, unsure if it was the stalker or someone trying to help. My heart raced as I debated my next move, feeling more vulnerable than ever.

"Aurora? Ro? Answer me. Are you alright?" Caleb called out from the other side of the door; his concern evident in his voice. Relief flooded me as I recognized his familiar tone, knowing I wasn't alone in this terrifying situation.

With a shaky hand, I slowly opened the door to let Caleb in, grateful for his presence in that moment of uncertainty. "Is someone here?"

"I am okay. I just thought I saw someone at my door when I arrived." I responded. Caleb grabbed me and pulled me close. His protective embrace provided a sense of security amid my fear. As we stood together, I couldn't help but feel grateful for his unwavering support during this unsettling experience.

"I don't understand, Aurora. You could easily handle someone like Luke." Caleb's voice was laced with concern as he searched my face. "You have been acting weird lately. What is going on?"

His words pierced through my carefully constructed facade, leaving me exposed and vulnerable. I tried to maintain my composure, but the unease swirling within me was difficult to conceal.

"What do you mean?" I asked, feigning ignorance. But Caleb wasn't fooled. His gaze remained fixed on me, his intuition telling him there was more to the situation than I was letting on.

"You can tell me anything, Aurora. I'm here for you," he reassured me, his voice gentle and sincere. "Aurora?"

The weight of my secret pressed down on me, threatening to crush my resolve. With a sigh of resignation, I finally relented.

"My powers were sealed," I admitted, my voice barely above a whisper. "Not completely, but enough that I cannot really control them anymore."

Caleb's expression softened as he listened to my explanation, his supportive presence providing me with a sense of comfort during this challenging time.

"I had no idea," he responded, his voice filled with empathy and understanding.

"Let's just say something happened, and the elders took it upon themselves to limit my abilities," I added, the bitterness in my voice betraying my frustration with the situation.

The elders' decision had left me feeling powerless and vulnerable, a shadow of my former self. And now, with Luke on the loose, I couldn't help but wonder if their actions had put us all at risk.

"I am sorry." He nodded, his eyes reflecting genuine concern.

I pulled back and asked, "Enough of that. What happened? Did you get him?"

"No, but we will find him." He replied, "But we are 100 percent sure it's him. Unfortunately, we found several victims. There were five of them. We also found a note in the middle of the living room floor and purple roses matching the ones you received." His words sent a chill down my spine, confirming my worst fears. The realization that the danger was closer than I had ever imagined made me cling to him even tighter, knowing we were together. So, it could have been him earlier at my door. I couldn't shake the feeling of unease, wondering how long he had been watching me. The thought of him being so close made me fear for my safety more than ever.

"I have you," Caleb whispered into my ear. "I will protect you. Have a seat. I will make you some tea."

I felt a wave of relief wash over me at his words, grateful for his presence in that moment of uncertainty. As he walked towards the kitchen to prepare the tea, I couldn't help but feel calm, knowing he was by my side. I stared at him from the table. Memories of us tonight are resurfacing. I remembered how we laughed and cuddled on the sofa while watching stupid TV shows. We would spend hours talking about everything and nothing. The warmth of his smile brought back a flood of nostalgia, reminding me of the bond we shared before everything changed. Looking at him, I could see that he stared back.

The weight of his stare pressed against my skin, a tangible force that sent shivers down my spine. Caleb. Even across the room, his gaze found me, a silent predator stalking its prey. I could feel the heat of his passion burning into me—a dangerous fascination that both thrilled and terrified me.

It had always been this way between us—a volatile dance of attraction and repulsion, love and hate. Our past was a tangled web of passion and pain, a love story gone wrong that had left us both scarred and yearning for something we couldn't have.

I tried to focus on the case—the cold facts and figures—in stark contrast to the simmering emotions swirling within me. But Caleb's presence was a constant distraction, a magnetic pull threatening to unravel my carefully constructed facade of indifference. Which, at the moment, was a good thing.

I knew he was watching me, analyzing my every move, trying to decipher the enigma of Aurora McCoy. He wanted to dominate me, mate me. I met his gaze from across the room, a silent challenge passing between us. He smirked, a predatory glint in his eyes, daring me to resist the inevitable. I refused to back down; my chin held high, and my eyes narrowed in defiance.

I knew the dangers of this game we were playing and the risks of succumbing to the dark desires that lurked beneath the surface of our strained relationship. But I couldn't deny the thrill of it all—the intoxicating rush of adrenaline that coursed through my veins whenever he was near.

I was a moth drawn to his flame, a deadly obsession that threatened to consume me whole. And as I stared back at him, a silent battle raging within me, I knew I was in for the fight of my life. One I was okay with losing to. This was no longer just a case to be solved; it was a mystery to be unraveled. This was personal—a battle of wills, a clash of two alpha personalities vying for dominance.

And as the tension between us reached a fever pitch, I couldn't help but wonder. If I would survive this case. Would I emerge from this case unscathed? Or would I become another casualty in the dangerous game of love and desire? We have to find and stop Luke no matter what.

Chapter 12

Caleb

There is something more to the look that Aurora is giving me. It's as if she can see right through me, into the depths of my soul. The intensity in her eyes is both unnerving and exhilarating. But behind those eyes, I know the fear she tries to hide. She doesn't think she will survive this case. I can sense her vulnerability, making me want to protect her even more. I need to find a way to reassure her that we will get through this together. Despite our relationship's past and complexities, we would face the darkness hand-in-hand.

The detective in her was already calculating and analyzing the risks and potential leads. But there was a flicker of something else in her eyes—hope, maybe even a hint of trust.

Trust that I wouldn't let her down, that I would protect her with my life, and that I would help her catch the monster who was terrorizing her. I wanted to pull her back into my arms to reassure her that I would never let anything happen to her. But I knew that words weren't enough. Actions were what mattered now.

I had to find a way to balance my duties as Alpha with my desire to keep her safe. I had to use every resource at my disposal—every connection, every instinct—to track down the killer and bring them to justice.

This wasn't just about protecting Aurora; it was about protecting my pack and my city. And it was about proving to myself and her that I could be the man she deserved.

As I watched her walk around, her silhouette outlined against the city lights, I made a silent vow. I would not fail her again. This time, I would be her shield, protector, and partner in this dangerous dance with death. And I would not rest until she was safe in my arms, the threat against her eradicated, and our love given a chance to bloom anew.

"Ro, talk to me," I say softly, gently touching her arm. "I'm here for you; we'll figure this out." Her eyes softened at my words, and I knew she understood we were together. Together, we will face whatever challenges come our way, united in our determination to overcome them. With her by my side, I feel invincible, ready to take on the world and protect the woman I love with all my heart.

"Caleb, I am scared. If what we know is true, I will be the twenty-eighth victim." Aurora whispers, her voice trembling with fear.

I take a deep breath, trying to find the right words to comfort her. "We will do everything we can to ensure that doesn't happen," I promised, squeezing her hand reassuringly.

"I think he is watching the house." Aurora's voice quivers as she shares her fear, her eyes darting nervously towards the window.

"We need to stay calm and focus," I reply, scanning the surroundings for any signs of danger.

"We can't let fear control us. We will get through this together. We must be vigilant and stick together until we devise a plan."

"Okay." She gives a little nod of her head. "I trust you."

"Let's ensure all the doors and windows are locked just to be safe," I suggest, keeping my voice steady despite the rising sense of unease. "We will get through this, Aurora. I won't let anything happen to you."

I got up and checked the doors and windows to ensure they were locked. As I moved around the room, I couldn't shake the feeling that we were being watched. I made a mental note to watch for any unusual activity outside. Officer Jenny Jones and Officer Jones Davis were watching the house. I will have to ask them if they have seen anything.

After checking the last window, I double- checked the locks and returned to Aurora, determined to stay strong for her. Walking back to the living room, where Aurora is, there was a knock on the door. I hesitated momentarily, wondering who it could be at this late hour. Taking a deep breath, I opened the door to find Officer Jones standing there, their expressions solemn. She informed me that they had spotted a suspicious individual lurking around the neighborhood and wanted to ensure we were safe. I thanked her for the warning and assured her we would be extra cautious.

"Officer Davis would like to have a word with you." Officer Jones informed me. I followed Officer Jones outside to where Officer Davis was waiting, feeling a sense of unease settle in the pit of my stomach.

"Did Officer Davis tell you why he needed to speak to me?" I questioned.

Officer Jones shook her head, her expression unreadable. "He didn't say, but I'm sure it's just a precaution." She replied reassuringly. I nodded, trying to push aside my growing sense of worry as we approached.

As I strode towards the idling patrol car, the early morning air hung heavy with the scent of damp asphalt and exhaust. A pang of unease tightened my gut. What could be so urgent that it warranted pulling me away from Aurora at this ungodly hour? Officer Jones, her typically brisk pace reduced to a measured trudge, trailed behind me, her face etched with a grimness that didn't bode well.

The cruiser's flashing lights painted grotesque shadows on the surrounding buildings, amplifying the already tense atmosphere. As we reached the car, a figure emerged from the driver's seat, their face obscured by the harsh glare of the headlights.

Before I could register their features or even utter a greeting, a sudden, blinding pain erupted in the back of my head. The world dissolved into a swirling vortex of darkness, and I crumpled to the pavement, consciousness slipping away like sand through my fingers.

Chapter 13

Aurora

What could Officer Davis want with Caleb at this hour? The question nags at me as he leaves with Officer Jones. A pang of unease tightened my gut. It was well past midnight. Whatever it is, it must be urgent for them to meet at this late hour. I couldn't shake the feeling that something was wrong.

I opened up the missing person database on my laptop to distract myself. As I scrolled through the profiles, my mind wandered back to Caleb and the mysterious meeting. I couldn't help but worry about what could be happening. The more I searched, the more anxious I became. Shaking my head, I continued with my search. Nothing was jumping out at me.

"Okay, Aurora. Take a breath." I whispered into the quiet room. I focused on one profile at a time, determined to find any possible lead to help me figure out the next victim or victims. We still have two more to go before I become the twenty-eighth victim. A particular name caught my eye as I dove deeper into the database and scrolled back in time. Olivia Marie Hudson. Olivia went missing one month ago. She fits the profile of the previous victims: young, with red-ish hair, and plus-size. My heart raced as I clicked on her profile, hoping to find a connection that could lead me to the killer. She was last seen at Randall Park Mall.

"Randall Park Mall. That is where I first met Caleb." I remembered the day clearly—it was a chance encounter that had changed the course of my life. The pieces were coming together, and I knew I was getting closer to solving the mystery. Could she be connected to the current case? I needed to dig deeper into Olivia's disappearance to see if any links could help solve this mystery. "Something about her strikes a chord of recognition within me. Why?" I asked, my voice filled with curiosity and a hint of confusion.

Opening up the video chat app, I sent the photo to Uncle Javier, hoping he could run the photo and video call him. I needed his expertise in facial recognition technology to see if Olivia's face matched anyone in the database. As I waited for his response, my mind raced with what this connection could mean for the case. As the call connected, I eagerly awaited his response, hoping he could provide insight into my connection with Olivia.

"Sorry, Ro. I was running facial recognition software." Uncle Javier said as he answered the call.

"Did you find a match?" I asked, my heart pounding with anticipation. Uncle Javier hesitated before responding, "Yes, Olivia's face matched with someone in the database. But you're not going to believe who it is. I am sending a team over now."

"Enough with the games, Uncle Javier, please." I pleaded, my voice trembling with impatience.

Uncle Javier sighed, "It's Officer Jenny Jones." My heart stopped as I processed his words, the connection with Olivia suddenly making sense in a way I never could have imagined. There was always something about her. It all clicked into place, the pieces of the puzzle falling together in my mind.

"Shit. Uncle Officer Jones just called Caleb out. He went with her." I said, feeling a sense of urgency creeping in. Uncle Javier's eyes widened in shock. I rushed to grab my phone, my mind racing with worry for Caleb. Uncle Javier quickly dialed Officer Davis, his expression grave as no one answered.

"Honey, sit down and do not open the door for anyone. I will be there soon. Safety safe." Uncle Javier said it firmly, his voice filled with concern. I nodded, my heart pounding with fear for Caleb's safety as I waited anxiously for Uncle Javier to arrive. I began pacing back and forth. My mind was consumed with worst-case scenarios, each more terrifying than the last. I prayed that Caleb would be okay and that Uncle Javier would arrive quickly to help.

A shrill ring of the phone jolted me from her thoughts. Impatiently, I reached for the phone and said, "McCoy."

"Detective McCoy, it's Officer Jones." My heart skipped a beat. The fact that Officer Jones was calling me meant that something serious had happened. My stomach churned with dread as I braced for the news she would deliver. This bitch.

"What's happened, Officer Jones?" I asked. The silence on the other end of the line was deafening, making my anxiety spike even higher. I'm getting tired of this cat-and-mouse game. "Officer Jones, I have a hunch Caleb is with you. Is he safe?" I asked, my voice barely above a whisper. The line remained silent for an eternity before a man's voice finally broke the silence. "Roses are purple, violets are blue," he said cryptically. My heart sank as I realized this was not a simple phone call; it was a message from Caleb's kidnapper. My heart sank as the reality of the situation hit me like a ton of bricks.

"Luke. What do you want?" I yelled at him through the phone.

The man on the other end chuckled darkly before replying, "I want you to play along if you ever want to see Caleb again." The dread in my stomach turned into a cold, paralyzing fear as I realized the dangerous game that was about to unfold.

"Luke," I said, my voice shaking slightly as I tried to maintain my composure. "You know this isn't the way to go about things. Whatever you want, we can work something out. Just tell me what you need and let Caleb go."

There was a long pause before Luke finally responded, his voice laced with amusement: "Oh, Detective McCoy, always so eager to negotiate. But this time, there's no negotiation. This is a game, and you'll play by my rules."

"What are your rules?" I asked, my voice barely a whisper.

"First rule: you do exactly as I say, no questions asked. The second rule: don't involve the police. Third rule: you come alone to the location I will give you."

I took a deep breath, trying to calm my racing heart. "And if I don't follow your rules?"

"Let's just say Caleb won't be seeing his next birthday," Luke said, his voice dripping with malice. "Now, listen carefully. I'm only going to say this once..."

I felt a chill run down my spine as I realized the seriousness of the situation. Luke had Caleb, and I had no choice but to comply with his demands if I wanted to see him again. The gravity of the situation sank in as I knew I had to act quickly and cautiously. With no time to waste, I braced myself for what lay ahead and prepared to do whatever it took to save Caleb. It was my fault that he was in this mess. I had to prepare myself for the dangerous game Luke was about to play, knowing that one wrong move could cost Caleb his life.

My heart raced as I steeled myself for the challenges ahead, determined to outsmart Luke and bring Caleb home safely. I know exactly what I had to do.

My mind was going a mile a minute. I knew I had to think fast and devise a plan to outsmart Luke before it was too late. With Caleb's life on the line, I had no choice but to play along for now and find a way to turn the tables on him later. I focused on every word Luke said, trying to devise a strategy to protect Caleb and myself.

The weight of the situation pressed down on me, but I knew I had to stay strong and think clearly to outmaneuver Luke's dangerous game. Caleb was an Alpha wolf, and I knew that his life was valuable to me and his entire pack. I couldn't let Luke's twisted game end in tragedy for us all. My heart raced as I tried to formulate a plan to outwit Luke and ensure Caleb's safety, knowing that failure was not an option.

As my mind raced, a sudden wave of intuition washed over me, a tingling sensation that I had learned to trust. It was as if the universe was sending me a message, a faint whisper of guidance amidst the chaos. I closed my eyes, focusing on the energy swirling around me, and a vision flashed before my eyes – a weathered pier stretching out into a moonlit lake, wind whipping through my hair fast, a silhouette, and the warmth of Caleb's embrace. I couldn't explain it, but I knew that this was the key to our survival. I just don't know what it means.

"Now, listen carefully. I'm only going to say this once. You'll find your first clue at the place where you first met Caleb. Be there in one hour, or the consequences will be dire. Tick-tock, Detective." The line went dead, leaving me in stunned silence. My mind raced as I tried to process his words. The place where I first met Caleb was Randall Park Mall. But it closed down.

I glanced at the clock; only fifty minutes remained. Panic started to set in, but I pushed it down. I couldn't afford to lose my cool. I had to focus on getting Caleb back. I grabbed my keys and rushed out of the house.

The drive to the lot where Randall Park Mall used to be a blur. I parked haphazardly and ran inside, my eyes scanning the parking lot for anything unusual. A small, folded piece of paper taped to the lamp post caught my eye. I snatched it up and unfolded it, my heart pounding.

It read, "Congratulations; you made it. Your next destination is the place where secrets are buried."

A chill ran down my spine. The place where secrets are buried? What could that mean? A cemetery? Caleb's mother and my mother were buried at the same cemetery. I quickly got back into my car, trying to piece together the clue in my mind. As I drove towards the nearest cemetery, my thoughts raced with the possibilities of what secrets awaited me there. The idea of uncovering buried secrets in a cemetery sent shivers down my spine.

As I navigated the winding roads, my mind raced with anticipation and fear of what I might discover. The sun was setting as I arrived at the cemetery, casting long shadows over the gravestones. I took a deep breath and prepared to uncover the secrets hidden within the silent grounds. The eerie silence of the cemetery only added to the suspense as I stepped out of my car and began to explore. Each gravestone seemed to hold a story waiting to be told, and I was determined to unravel the mystery that had brought me there.

I strolled through the rows of gravestones, each inscription a reminder of a life lived, and a story left behind. The air grew thicker as the darkness descended, casting long, ominous shadows over the graves. I shivered, not from the cold but from a deep-seated unease that had settled in my bones.

My eyes scanned the names on the headstones, hoping for a sign or a clue. And then, I saw it. My mother's grave. A wave of sadness washed over me as I kneeled beside it, tracing the letters of her name with my fingers.

As I reached around the headstone, my hand brushed against something cold and metallic. My heart leaped into my throat as I pulled back the foliage to reveal a small metal box half-buried in the dirt. I carefully unearthed it, my hands trembling with anticipation.

The box was old and rusted, with a simple latch. I pried it open, and another piece of paper was nestled amongst a few faded photographs of me and Caleb and trinkets I didn't recognize. My heart pounded as I unfolded it, eager to decipher the next clue.

The message was short and chilling this time: "The final piece of the puzzle awaits where your time stood still."

I racked my brain, recalling when time stood still for me and/or Caleb. Suddenly, it hit me—Pier W. The last place we were together. I knew I had to return to Pier W., where Caleb and I had shared a special moment. It was a moment frozen when I mustered the courage to accept his proposal and resist the urge to flee from him. As I rushed to the location, memories flooded back, guiding me toward the final puzzle piece hidden in that nostalgic spot.

I sped through the dimly lit streets, my mind racing with a mix of dread. Pier W was a secluded spot overlooking the water, where Caleb and I often went for dinner. My heart pounded as I parked the car and made my way there.

The air was still and heavy with the scent of the sea; the only sound was the gentle lapping of waves against the shore. There they stood. The two figures, silhouetted against the moonlit water, turned towards me as I approached. Officer Jenny Jones (or Olivia Hudson) and Luke.

Chapter 14

Aurora

"Look who made it in time," Luke comments. I could feel the tension rising as I braced myself for the conversation that was about to unfold. The moonlight cast a surreal glow on their faces, adding to the moment's intensity.

"Look who we have here, Officer Jones. Or should I call you Olivia?" I responded. The tension in the air was palpable as I tried to maintain my composure. My heart raced as I waited for their next move, unsure of what would happen next.

"Look who is good at their job." Officer Jones says. I could sense a hint of sarcasm in her voice, making me even more on edge.

"Cut the act, Officer Jones." I said, trying to assert my authority despite the unease creeping in.

"Now, now, ladies. Let's all calm down and talk this out like civilized people," Luke interrupted, breaking the tension in the room.

"What is it that you desire, Luke?" I inquired.

"I desire you," Luke replied, his eyes narrowing as he spoke. "And I won't stop until I get you."

"Why, Luke?" I asked. "Why me? Why betray Caleb?"

Luke's expression darkened, his gaze unwavering. "Because you're worth it," he said with a chilling smile. His words sent a shiver down my spine as I realized the depth of his obsession.

"You never even talked to me," I replied.

"I've been watching you, studying you from afar," Luke confessed. "And I know that we're meant to be together." His intensity made me uneasy as I tried to find a way to diffuse the situation.

"That doesn't explain why you are killing women who look like me." I comment.

Luke's smile faded, replaced by a cold, calculating look. "They tried to replace you," he said softly. The realization that I was in grave danger hit me like a ton of bricks, and I knew I had to find a way to escape before it was too late.

"But you kept Officer Jones, I mean Olivia, alive." I respond.

Luke's expression darkened even further at the mention of Olivia. "She was different," he muttered, sending shivers down my spine. The fear in his eyes told me that I needed to act quickly if I wanted to survive this twisted game he was playing. "She wanted to help me get you."

"Where is Caleb?" I demanded, my voice echoing with the urgency of a cornered animal.

"It is always about Caleb with you." Luke spat, his voice dripping with venom. "You see no one else but him. He was never good for you. He wouldn't even choose you over the pack." His words twisted like daggers, piercing the fragile hope I had held onto. "I was there when you cried because of him. But did you see me? No."

The pain of his accusations caused a wave of rage to wash over me. "Why now? Why mention this now?" I retorted, my voice rising. "Why kill all those women? To what end? To make me notice you?"

Luke's eyes burned with a mixture of rage and hurt. "I did it because I love you." He confessed; his voice raw with emotion. "And I will do anything to prove that I'm the one who truly cares for you."

My heart pounded against my ribs as I struggled to comprehend the depth of his twisted obsession. The thought of someone taking innocent lives to gain my attention filled me with a bone- chilling dread.

Yet, I couldn't let fear control me. I had to maintain my composure to find a way out of this dangerous situation.

Summoning my inner strength, I reached deep within myself, calling upon the ancient magic that flowed through my veins. A flicker of power ignited in my eyes, a silent warning to the man before me. "Luke." I began, my voice steady despite the turmoil, "Your actions are not born of love but madness. True love doesn't seek to harm or control. It seeks to nurture and protect."

A cold shiver ran down my spine as I realized the true extent of his depravity. He had not only taken innocent lives but had also kidnapped a young girl, a chilling reminder of the darkness that lurked beneath the surface. I knew then that I couldn't reason with him and had to fight for my survival and the safety of the innocent.

"Luke." I began to say, but the sudden appearance of a gun in his hand cut me short. My mind raced, desperately searching for a way to defuse the volatile situation. Realizing that his love had twisted into something dangerous and unstable, I shivered.

"No more talking." Luke's voice was firm, his eyes reflecting a dangerous mix of anger and desperation. I knew I had to remain calm to find a way out of this nightmare.

Taking a deep breath, I met his gaze with a steady resolve. "I was just going to say you should have told me," I admitted, my voice barely above a whisper. "I like you too." It was a gamble, a desperate attempt to connect with the man I thought I knew.

The tension in the room eased slightly as Luke's grip on the gun loosened. A flicker of hope ignited within me, a belief that perhaps there was still a chance for a peaceful resolution.

"I know I should have said something sooner." I continued, my voice gaining strength. "But I was afraid. Afraid of how you might react and what it might mean for us."

I watched as the conflict in Luke's eyes intensified, his emotions warring within him. It was a risky move, but I knew that honesty and vulnerability were my only weapons against the darkness that threatened to consume him.

Slowly, I extended my hand towards him, my fingers brushing against the cold metal of the gun. "Luke, please," I whispered, my voice filled with fear and hope. "Let's talk about this. Let's find a way out of this together."

As our hands touched, a surge of disgust coursed through me, but I pushed it aside. I'm hoping Luke believes my lies. I needed to keep him talking and distracted long enough for help to arrive. The tension in the room was suffocating, but I had to stay strong for both of us. At that precise moment, Luke's eyes lost their glimmer of doubt and replaced it with one of love.

Unbeknownst to me, the inherited witch magic within me stirred, responding to the emotional intensity of the moment. It enveloped me in a protective shield, a silent testament to the power that lay dormant within my bloodline.

"Please, Luke, trust me." I pleaded; my voice infused with the magic that flowed through me.

For a fleeting moment, the tension in the room dissipated. Luke's expression softened, and a single tear rolled down his cheek. He finally nodded, his grip on the gun loosening further.

Emboldened by his response, I whispered a prayer to my ancestors, calling upon their wisdom and strength.

"Luke, let's build a life together," I repeated, and the taste of vomit filled my mouth. "Let's leave this all behind and start anew."

Tears welled up in Luke's eyes as he lowered the gun, a trembling smile forming on his lips. But before relief could thoroughly wash over me, his eyes darkened again, the warmth replaced by a cold, vacant stare.

A loud bang shattered the fragile peace. Followed by two more deafening shots. Time seemed to distort as I watched in horror, my protective shield collapsing under the onslaught. Luke's body crumpled to the ground, lifeless, and the echoes of the gunshots mocked my desperate attempts to save myself.

Pain seared through my chest as I fell beside him, the realization of my own mortality crashing over me. There was one piece of information I forgot. The silhouette I saw in my vision. It was the one detail that could have saved us both. Now, as darkness closed in around me, I knew it was too late to escape the consequences of my oversight.

I turned to the side to see Officer Jenny Jones bleeding. Or, Olivia Marie Hudson. How could I have forgotten about you? She managed to sneak up behind me and deliver a fatal blow, her eyes filled with a mix of triumph and pain before they went blank. Luke shot her, and she retaliated, taking him down with her.

The sirens wailed in the distance, a chilling reminder that my story was nearing its tragic end. I wish my magic hadn't been sealed. If only it had been more powerful, perhaps I would have had a chance at survival had someone come to my aid in time. Tears streamed down my face as I whispered a final goodbye to Caleb. If I could go back in time, I would be your wife and live a peaceful life away from all this chaos. But as I felt the darkness closing in, I knew it was too late for regrets.

The world grew dim around me, the sirens fading into a distant hum. I could hear someone calling my name, but it was too late. The darkness enveloped me, and as I closed my eyes, accepting my fate, the last thing I heard was Caleb's voice, filled with anguish and love. "I lo...ve...yo..u..." I echoed, my voice barely a whisper, as the darkness claimed me.

www.ingramcontent.com/pod-product-compliance
Lightning Source LLC
Chambersburg PA
CBHW030007010826
48973CB00009B/2703